BLACKSTONE ON BROADWAY

BLACKSTONE ON BROADWAY

RICHARD FALKIRK

THISTLE
PUBLISHING

To Peter and Marie Pateman,
owners of the magnificent
Blackstone Room Restaurant
in the Jamaica Inn, Denia, Alicante, Spain

AUTHOR'S NOTE

I have tried to make the historical background to this novel as accurate as possible. I have, however, indulged some literary licence and made adjustments to chronology, to make Blackstone's visit to Manhattan more colourful. The period is loosely 1820–30, the decade which Edmund Blackstone bestrides. Many of the characters, such as the High Constable, Jacob Hays, did exist; others are fictitious.

The plot is based on the story, regarded by many authorities as a hoax, of a lawsuit brought by Frederic Law Olmsted against various members of the Astor family, documented in *Studies in Early American History,* which was privately published in Chicago in 1897. Olmsted was reported to have laid a claim of five million dollars against the Astors, on behalf of one of his ancestors, who had been given Deer Isle in 1699 by Indians of the Penobscot tribe. The charge was that a trader working for the Astors had found Captain Kidd's box on the island and that they had appropriated its contents, the treasure. A disclaimer was later circulated, saying that one Franklin Head, documentor of the lawsuit, had fabricated the whole story. In other words Mr Head had only been *Kidding.* Or had he?

CHAPTER ONE

The Ruby lay in the palm of Edmund Blackstone's hand, stirring his senses like the touch of a seductress.

He felt its warmth, gazed into its slumbrous fires. Lust expanded inside him, the hunger of the treasure hunter scenting his prey.

'Well?' The skinny little man with the starved face and greedy eyes looked at him eagerly.

'It's a beautiful stone,' Blackstone admitted cautiously, keeping tight rein on his lust.

'Beautiful? It's exquisite, finer than any stone in the Crown Jewels.' The jeweller nibbled at some dry skin on his bottom lip. 'What do you say? Are you game?'

Blackstone placed the ruby on the mahogany table. It lay between the Bow Street Runner and the jeweller, as warm as blood in a shaft of spring sunlight. What was its history? How many men had fought and died for it? How many women had sold themselves for it? For a moment Blackstone thought he sensed its malignant power. Then, annoyed at his lapse of sanity, he took some snuff and directed his irritation towards the jeweller.

'Where was it pinched from?'

The jeweller, whose name was Fogarty, nibbled excitedly. 'It wasn't stolen, it was *found*.'

'Where was it *found*? In the Jewel House at the Tower?'

'I told you where it was found – in America.'

'You'll have to do better than that, culley.' Blackstone placed his Bow Street baton beside the ruby. 'A few more details please, Mr Fogarty. How did it come into your possession?'

Fogarty's head bobbed on his thin neck; beneath the shabby clothes, Blackstone surmised, his body was probably girded by a money belt.

'It was brought to me by a client.'

'Ah.' Blackstone nodded understandingly. 'A dodger?'

Fogarty looked puzzled.

'A dodgy character. Flash, was he?'

'He wasn't my usual sort of client,' Fogarty admitted. 'You know, I only deal with the better class of person ...' His voice faltered as he saw the controlled anger on Blackstone's face.

'Bit of a snob, aren't you, Mr Fogarty. Would you consider me to be *a better class of person?*' Blackstone held up his hand to cut off the reply. 'What you mean is that you only deal with swells until some cracksman comes along with a ruby as big as a chicken's egg.'

Fogarty mustered a scrap of dignity and said: 'I did summon a Bow Street Runner immediately the ruby came into my possession.'

'Aye, that you did. But not in an official capacity. In a strictly private one, eh, Mr Fogarty?' Blackstone stood up and stretched. 'I may have to take you down to Bow Street for further questioning.'

Fogarty drew blood on his lower lip. 'You wouldn't—'

'I would.'

'Haven't you any morals?'

'Morals?' Blackstone looked quizzically at the little jeweller. 'Have you a dictionary handy, Mr Fogarty? Morals is a word I haven't come across. You see,' he said, 'I was brought up in the Rookery and morals wasn't a word they taught us, because we weren't *a better class of person*. Thieving, milling, coining – yes, morals – no. And in any case,' Blackstone went on, 'wasn't it my lack of morals – whatever they may be – that made you send for me?'

'I sent for you', Fogarty said, 'because I had heard you were a swashbuckling sort of character willing to undertake any dangerous mission. After all, the King chose you to sail to St Helena to stop Napoleon escaping.'*

'Correction,' Blackstone said, picking up the baton and pointing it at Fogarty. 'You sent for me because you think the Bow Street Runners are a band of rogues protected by the law. You sent for me because you had heard that I only crossed the border to the right side of the law by chance and I could be persuaded to return. Am I right, Mr Fogarty?' Blackstone asked, deciding that, divested of his clothes, the jeweller would resemble a plucked chicken.

'No, sir, you are not.'

'Come off it, culley,' Blackstone said. 'You're a bit of a fence on the side, aren't you?' He leaned across the table. 'Now let's have the truth, Mr Fogarty. Where did that ruby come from? Come clean with me and I *may* accept that you're helping the law.'

Nervously, Fogarty related his story. A hotel thief – 'A snoozer,' Blackstone interrupted – had come to him with the ruby, asking 'an outrageous price'. Fogarty had paid him a fifth of the asking-price and had immediately summoned Blackstone. It was the first time that he had made such a transaction.

---

* See *Blackstone and the Scourge of Europe*.

'Of course,' Blackstone said. 'Now, some more details. Where did he pinch the ruby?'

'In the George and Vulture in Lombard Street.'

'And who did he lift it from?'

'An American sea captain. That's why I said it was found in America.'

'And who was the dodgy little snoozer, Mr Fogarty. Was he flash or just a gonoph?'

Fogarty said hesitantly: 'I think he was a little scared by the value of the ruby.'

'Do you know his name?'

Fogarty shook his head.

'A description please, Mr Fogarty.'

Fogarty gazed at the ruby imprisoning the rays of the sun in its blood-red heart. 'Very tall, greying hair on the greasy side, wearing a black velveteen coat, a grey hat with mildew on it and a red handkerchief at his throat. And he stuttered,'

Fogarty added.

'A stuttering snoozer!' Blackstone grinned. 'Shouldn't be too difficult to find. Unless, of course, the Yankee skipper has reported the loss, in which case it won't be necessary. If he hasn't,' – Blackstone looked thoughtful – 'then the case becomes very interesting...'

'What I want to know', Fogarty said, 'is whether you're game or not?'

'And what I want to know', Blackstone said, 'is why you told me the ruby is part of a treasure trove.'

'If I confide in you, can I be sure the information won't be used against me?'

Blackstone said mildly: 'You can only be sure of one thing: if you don't confide in me, you'll spend the night in a cell at Bow Street.'

Fogarty licked the blood from his lip. 'Very well, I'll trust you. There is a certain camaraderie in my profession. You know, we exchange information so that we can report stolen property for publication in the *Hue and Cry*.' He gazed earnestly at Blackstone. He was rewarded with an expression of theatrical cynicism and carried on hastily: 'Anyway, it seems that there have been three precious stones circulating in London recently which have apparently all come from the same source in America. New York, in fact. And it's my belief that the source is a single hoard of treasure. You see, Blackstone, I'm something of an authority on treasure troves.' His skeletal features became animated. 'At the moment I 'm on the track of some of the stones stolen from the Chamber of the Pyx in Westminster Abbey in 1303—'

'Let's confine ourselves to the ruby,' Blackstone interrupted. 'Why do you think it comes from the same source as the other three stones?'

'A hunch, Blackstone. A hunch backed by a certain amount of evidence. You see, the other three were all set in Arabian gold.'

'So?'

'Don't you see? They must have been loot from the old Red Sea trade. Two hundred years ago the east coast ports of North America did a great trade with the pirates. Their ships, laden with cannon, stores and rum, sailed round the Cape of Good Hope and met the privateers in the Indian Ocean, where the cargo was exchanged for jewels and spice and Arabian gold.' Fogarty was drooling now. 'And then they sailed back to America, where no one asked any questions.'

Lust slavered inside Blackstone again. 'Why should this ruby' – he picked it up and caressed it – 'have any connection with Arabian gold?'

'If I tell you, will you carry out the mission? Will you sail to New York and find out the source of the ruby?'

Blackstone grinned at him. 'Anything's possible, Mr Fogarty. And if you don't tell me, the very least you can expect for receiving stolen property is transportation to Van Diemen's Land, where they give you fifty lashes for receiving a grain of corn.'

Fogarty nibbled excitedly. 'Very well,' he said, opening a drawer in the table with trembling hands and taking out a scroll of parchment. 'This is a copy of the inventory of a vessel named the *Quedah*.'

Blackstone glanced at the list and asked Fogarty to explain.

Fogarty said: 'The three stones set in Arabian gold all correspond to items on that list. And so does the ruby.'

Blackstone ran his finger down the list. 'There's an item here referring to *two* rubies.'

'Aye. Identical twins – and I 've got one of them. I want the other and I want the rest of the treasure that goes with it.'

'Tell me about the *Quedah*.'

'The *Quedah* was an Armenian merchant ship that was captured on 30 January 1698.'

'Really? And who captured her?'

'Captain Kidd,' Fogarty said.

The American sea captain had not reported the theft of the ruby, so there was only one course open to Blackstone: find the stuttering snoozer!

It had been a fine morning and some of its hope lingered into the afternoon. Mounted on his horse, Poacher, Blackstone smelt the breezes from the river and enjoyed the butterfly colours of spring – the pastel shades of the new dresses worn by tiny-waisted girls in poke bonnets, the bolder hues of the dandies' coats, the gold and scarlet uniform of a little black boy standing on the back of his master's carriage. Fresh buds on the plane trees and the pale blue sky high above the confusion of roof-tops.

This was spring in the grand avenues of London; in Piccadilly, the Strand, Regent Street, St James's and St George's; in palace gardens and parks where daffodils grew. But Blackstone was heading towards areas where spring went unobserved, to the stews of the city where the sky was an occasional gap between leaning tenements, and hope ... what was hope?

Blackstone, in fact, was returning to his first home. And, as he approached the dung-heaps and twopenny lodging houses and thieves' kitchens and festering whorehouses of St Giles Rookery, the Holy Land, his spirits fled back to winter.

But this was where Blackstone gathered the information that had made him the second most feared Runner, after the ageing Townsend. Here he was hated and feared and respected because he had once been one of them, before he renegaded; because he knew their secrets and he could betray or reward them according to his whim.

Blackstone moved from daylight into dusk. He was inside the Rookery. He checked his two horse-pistols and the new Manton percussion in his belt.

His first contact, as always, was the one-eyed pieman.

A stuttering snoozer? The pieman's single eye glittered with amusement. 'He wouldn't stand much chance stuttering in the Rookery, Blackie. They'd cut his throat before he had time to plead for his life.'

In the background hollow-eyed urchins gathered to behold the big, swarthy Runner on his noble horse.

Blackstone liked to think that they sensed his friendship, that they guessed that the only men he wanted to dispatch to the hulks were their masters, who turned them into precocious slaves.

The pieman said: 'Why not try the Whistling Lad? He's just done a tour of likely haunts of your cove. The Devil's Acre, Seven Dials, Ratcliffe Highway. But best give him a sprat first, Blackie, or he'll warn every thief within miles with his whistle. Come to think of it,' said the pieman, worrying his blind socket with a grimy finger, 'I could do with a sprat to buy some more flour.'

Blackstone gave him six pennies and tossed a handful of coins to the urchins. 'Where's the Lad whistling these days?'

The pieman put a finger to his lips. 'Can't you hear him?'

Faintly, above the gabble of the street vendors and the shrieks of the urchins, Blackstone heard the whistling. *Will You Love Me Then As Now?*

Blackstone thanked the pieman and urged Poacher towards the thin notes of the song.

The Whistling Lad was a middle-aged, red-haired man who earned his living whistling ballads on his pitch at Covent Garden or in villages such as Highgate and Paddington, on the outskirts of London. He supplemented his living by acting as a crow, or look-out, for thieves, whistling a prearranged song to warn the cracksmen of danger; for this reason Blackstone tethered his horse and approached the Whistling Lad from behind.

Blackstone tapped the Whistling Lad on the back: the whistling stopped as though his vocal chords had been severed. 'What can I do for you, Blackie?' the Whistling Lad asked, his cheeks – hollowed from a lifetime of whistling – working like bellows.

Blackstone told him he was looking for the hotel thief.

The Whistling Lad looked blank, his lips still pursed. It was said that wherever he went he was followed by larks and thrushes and that with a few cajoling notes from his lips he could make a dumb cage-bird sing. He wore a Robin Hood hat with a jay's feather in it; he was experiencing pain in his lungs and had been advised to drink more beer to ward off consumption.

Blackstone gave him a gentle prod with his gilt-crowned baton. 'Come on, you know the whereabouts of every prig in town.' Blackstone glanced at an adjacent building bearing the sign LOGINS FOR WEARY TRAVELERS and added thoughtfully: 'Are you acting as crow right now, by any chance? Can't be many pickings for whistling here in the Rookery.'

The Whistling Lad emitted the first note of a ballad but Blackstone clamped his hand round his mouth. 'None of that, culley. Let's not disturb the coves in there just yet.'

The Whistling Lad looked as scared as a canary confronted by a cat. 'I ain't doing no harm, Blackie. Honest.'

'Of course you're not,' Blackstone agreed. 'Now why not whistle another verse of *Will You Love Me Then As Now?* That'll keep them happy, won't it, Whistler?' Blackstone prodded him again with his baton. 'Go on, whistle.'

Unhappily, the Whistling Lad obeyed and from the slit of sky a blackbird descended and perched on a line of sooty washing.

'That's enough,' Blackstone said. 'Now tell me where I can find the snoozer.'

'I don't know, Blackie. You know me, I'm not one to blab.'

'True, true. But I don't think the coves in there' – Blackstone pointed at the lodging house – 'would be too fond of you if they thought you'd betrayed them, now would they?'

The Whistling Lad's cheeks sank into deeper hollows. 'You're a hard man, Blackie.'

'Where's my little snoozer?'

The Whistling Lad gazed anxiously at the lodging house, hesitated and said: 'If I tell, will you scarper?'

'I just might,' Blackstone said.

'I hear tell there's a tea-leaf who stammers who's got a place down the Highway. Number twenty-three, I believe.'

Blackstone grinned. 'Thank you, Whistler. How's business, by the way?'

'Not so bloomin' good, Blackie. Lucky if I earns a shilling a day. Even the swells seem broke these days. Lucky if I gets enough blunt to buy a pint of ale for my lungs...'

Blackstone slipped him a sovereign. 'Here, buy yourself a barrel.'

From the lodging house there came the sound of a commotion, as though the thieves had been disturbed. Blackstone slipped away; the premises were owned by a landlord who had installed furniture from a smallpox hospital and crammed children into the tiny rooms at a penny a night. Blackstone couldn't think of a more worthy subject to be robbed.

As he rode away on Poacher he was accompanied by the whistling of a sailor's hornpipe, as cheery as the song of a lark in a green field.

Blackstone arrived at Ratcliffe Highway at dusk, as the lamplighter was attending to the new gas lamps. This was where seamen went hunting for girls, of whom there were plenty, and he himself was now dressed in a blue reefer jacket and flared trousers; he walked with a rolling gait and smoked a stubby clay pipe.

The Highway was already lively, teeming with pimps and prostitutes, pickpockets and rampsmen, drunken sailors lurching from the taverns as though fighting a gale on a heaving deck.

Blackstone sauntered past number twenty-three, a tavern with a dance hall and lodging rooms above; from one of these a bare-breasted girl smiled and beckoned. Blackstone walked on, heading for the White Swan, known as Paddy's Goose, the tavern seamen dreamed about in hot and distant ports.

Above the flare of the lamps, the sky was pricked with stars and he could smell the water of the Thames, the lifeblood of London.

The scene in Paddy's Goose was normal. A fight in one corner, a young boy dressed as a girl singing on a small stage, a crew of seamen with tankards in their paws, the tarts and their flash-carriers, dollymops who had come east on their monthly day off to earn a few shillings because you couldn't afford much finery on seven pounds a year, a few swells slumming, guarded by retired pugilists, the usual collection of pickpockets, speelers, mutchers and lurking footpads eager to relieve the sailors of their pay.

Blackstone ordered himself a grog and was immediately joined by a girl wearing a low-cut dress, mauve stockings and a pair of lace-up boots with high metal heels. She was about seventeen, with long black hair and a beauty spot on one cheek.

She smiled at Blackstone: 'Buy a girl a drink, Jack?'

'Why not?' said Blackstone, ordering her twopennyworth of gin.

'I thought I'd get in fast. A fellow with your sort of looks would have the girls after you like bees round a honeypot.'

'And the fellows would be blind not to be swarming round you.'

The beauty spot bobbed and curtsied her thanks. 'Who's your money on?' she asked, nodding towards the brawl between an Irishman with fists like turnips and a lascar.

'I always back a Paddy when it comes to milling,' Blackstone told her, watching the clubbing fists and waiting for the lascar to draw his knife.

'Done a bit of milling yourself, culley?'

Blackstone spat on one fist. 'A bit,' he said, modestly.

'Here, have a drink on me.' She hoisted her skirt, found her purse and tossed a coin to the barman.

One doctored drink coming up, Blackstone thought. He took the tankard, stumbled against a waterman standing beside him and spilled the ale. 'Lor,' he exclaimed, 'I'm as clumsy as an ox.'

The girl frowned. 'Let me get you another.'

Blackstone shook his head. 'Don't worry. How about coming down the road for a bit of a dance?'

The girl eyed him speculatively. This was her pitch and she was loath to leave it.

Blackstone played the card which couldn't be trumped. 'Come on, we'll have a good time – I've just been paid.'

'You've got a silver tongue,' she said, giggling and slipping her arm into his.

As they left, the lascar's knife glinted in the tobacco smoke like a silver fish. It was sent flying by a turnip-sized fist and the lascar fled for the door.

The dance hall above the tap-room at number twenty-three was furnished with deal tables and benches surrounding a bare-board floor, the knots brightly polished by scuffling feet. At one end of the room a four-piece band thumped out waltzes and polkas, while seamen and girls with skirts flying spun around and waiters in white aprons balanced tankards of ale on trays held high above their heads.

Blackstone and the girl sat at a table vacated by a Dutch sailor who had just been carried out feet first minus his wallet. Blackstone ordered two tankards of ale and turned to the girl. 'Been here before?'

'Once or twice. But I prefers Paddy's.'

'Do you live on the Highway?'

'Ask a lot of questions, don't you, culley,' the girl said, blowing the froth from her ale. She leaned forward suddenly and kissed him. 'When did you say you were last at sea, Jack? I don't taste no salt there. Usually when I kiss a bloke home from the sea I can taste the salt...'

'Perhaps they don't bath as often as me,' Blackstone said. And to change the subject he pointed upstairs and asked: 'What goes on up there?'

'The usual. Want to dab it up—?' She hesitated. 'What's your name, culley?'

'Whitestone,' Blackstone said. 'Samuel Whitestone.'

'Want to dab it up, Sam?'

'Let's have a dance first.'

He led her on to the floor and they careered round the room to the latest polka. When they returned to the table she was laughing and panting and saying: 'You certainly know how to give a girl a good time, Sam. Not like the others who just want a tumble. Not that there's anything wrong with that, mind, but it's nice to enjoy yourself in other ways. 'And when Blackstone had bought her a gin she continued: 'You know, it's nice to know that a fine, upstanding fellow like yourself likes my company, not just my...You know what I mean.' Blackstone could have sworn that she blushed.

A couple of gins later he asked casually: 'Does anyone live in those rooms upstairs?'

'A few coves, I've heard. The waiters I think. Do you feel like going up?' She looked at him shyly and Blackstone peered through the rouge and powder and saw what might have been. 'You know, I don't want blunt or anything like that. Not with you, Sam.'

'There's plenty of time,' Blackstone told her, thinking: But not for you. In a couple of years time you'll be a hag, enticing seamen down the alleys to be rumbled by a rampsman.

A new waiter had materialised beside them. Blackstone turned to him and said: 'A tankard of ale and another gin, please.' But he coughed as he spoke, so that the order was indistinct.

The waiter bent down. 'I d ... d ... didn't quite c ... c ... catch that, sir,' he said.

Half an hour later Blackstone made his move. He said to the girl, who was now a little drunk: 'Wait here a minute. I've got some business to attend to.'

She looked at him anxiously. 'You will be back, Sam?'

'Of course. Here, hold this in trust for me.' He handed her his snuff-box.

'You mean you trust me with that?'

And Blackstone, who knew that she had never been trusted with anything before, nodded. Then he went after the stuttering snoozer, who was heading for the tap-room below with a trayful of empty tankards.

Blackstone had almost reached the thief-cum-waiter when a gonoph who acted as an informant for Blackstone said in a loud voice: 'Strike me blind, it's Blackstone, What brings you to these parts, culley?'

All talk within a radius of five yards stopped. The waiter turned, stared at Blackstone for a moment, dropped his tray and made for the door. The throng opened for him, closed for Blackstone. Blackstone fought his way to the door and looked up and down the gas-lit street. He saw the waiter running in the direction of Paddy's Goose and gave chase. Thief and pursuer were a common enough sight on Ratcliffe Highway and no one took much notice.

Halfway to the tavern the waiter disappeared. When Blackstone reached the spot he found a dark alley leading away to the left; only a fool or a drunkard would venture down there alone. Blackstone drew a pocket pistol from his reefer jacket and proceeded cautiously. Rats scuttled away from him and in the shadows he could hear the sounds of the street girls earning their keep.

The alley smelt of rotting vegetables. Candles burned at a few windows; the rest were dark and dead, and even the pools of moonlight seemed stagnant. Blackstone thought he heard a movement a little way ahead; he tightened his grip on the pistol. Then he saw the waiter darting across a patch of moonlight. Blackstone followed, thinking – as he had often thought before – that it was a sight more danger-ous being on the right side of the law than it was across the border. He kept on the dark side of a broken-down fence, waiting for a shot or the swish of a cudgel in the night air.

When it happened it was unexpected, because it didn't involve Blackstone.

A thud, a cry, the sound of a body falling.

Blackstone ran forward.

A figure crouched over a body.

Blackstone shouted, the figure looked up. 'What the—?'

'Bow Street!' Blackstone shouted. 'Don't move, culley, or I'll blow your head off.'

But the figure moved, straightened up, ran. Blackstone aimed the pistol and fired. The alley was momentarily lit up by the explosion; rats, cats and humans at furtive play were frozen – then fled, following the man who had escaped the ball from Blackstone's pistol.

Blackstone knelt beside the snoozer. His head had been caved in by a blow from a cudgel and he would stutter no more.

Blackstone straightened up. The alley was quiet now and as peaceful as the moonlight. Blackstone swore. The dangerous classes had won a round; a footpad had killed one of his own kind and halted the processes of justice. Or thwarted an adventurer with the scent of treasure in his nostrils?

Thoughtfully, Blackstone made his way back to the Highway and cut through another alley to the back of number twenty-three. He opened a door and climbed the back stairs, past the dance hall to the rooms above.

The girl who had beckoned him opened a door and beckoned again. She was quite naked, but older than she had seemed from the street. Blackstone whispered 'Later', put his finger to his lips and quietly closed the door in her face.

Which room did you inhabit, poor dead stuttering snoozer? He opened one door, apologised to the couple on the bed, and moved on.

The third door he tried was locked. Blackstone took a skeleton key and picklock from his pocket and knelt down. Two minutes later the door swung open. In the moonlight pouring through the window he saw an unmade bed, a wardrobe, a table and a chair. He opened the wardrobe – a few poor clothes and a pair of shoes laced with string. Poor, amateurish snoozer, a gonoph who had graduated to looting hotel rooms and had made the fatal mistake of chancing upon a ruby that was too rich for him.

Blackstone closed the wardrobe and moved to the table. There was a bag on the table, locked. Blackstone attended to it with his instruments and found inside their twins – skeleton keys, picklock and a pair of outside pliers for grasping the tip of a key and turning it inside a lock.

But there was something else. A wallet. Blackstone exclaimed aloud and took it to the window. The wallet was pigskin and bore the imprint of a New York manufacturer; the moonlight turned to silver, the stars were diamonds.

Blackstone rifled the wallet. Ship's papers, an inventory, a letter written in bold handwriting, a locket containing a few strands of hair... But it was the papers that interested Blackstone, each bearing the name John Maudling, ship's captain. A few addresses in New York, one in Southampton and two in London, one of which was the George and Vulture. Blackstone slipped the wallet into his pocket and left the late snoozer's room, closing the door gently behind him.

The girl was still waiting at the table, tears gathering in her eyes. She blinked away the tears when Blackstone sat down beside her. 'I thought you'd gone for good, Sam.'

Blackstone fished two sovereigns from his pocket. 'I've got to go now. Here, take these.'

'I don't want them,' she said. 'Put them away.'

Blackstone took her hand, put the sovereigns in it and closed her fingers around them. 'Till next time,' he said.

He stood up to leave and the girl said: 'Haven't you forgotten something?' She handed him the snuff-box. 'You see, you trusted me.'

Blackstone smiled down at her. 'And I was right to, wasn't I?' he said. He kissed her gently on the forehead, then turned and walked away.

CHAPTER TWO

A nother fine, delicately-textured spring day. But in the office of Sir Richard Birnie, the Bow Street Magistrate, who didn't acknowledge the passing of winter till Midsummer's Day, a fire burned in the grate. And his mood was deep January.

There were several reasons why his gloom was even more firmly entrenched than usual. On the other side of Bow Street he could see one of Peel's day patrols lounging against the wall of the Brown Bear Tavern, chatting to two serving girls. Moronic flunkeys, Birnie brooded, noting their blue coats and trousers, black felt hats and red waistcoats. The Home Secretary, Sir Robert Peel, had introduced the patrols in 1822, ostensibly as an enlargement of the Runners, but the disguise was wearing thin and Birnie knew that, before the twenties were spent, Peel would try and form his own police force, just as he had formed the Peelers in Ireland.

But I'll fight him, Birnie reaffirmed, biting on the stem of his churchwarden pipe. By God, I'll fight him. And standing at the window of his spartan office he wondered whether he could have the popinjay patrol arrested for loitering with intent.

From the door of the Brown Bear three Runners emerged. Ruthven, built like a prizefighter, with his brains in his fists; Townsend, wily and arrogant, with money in the bank that Peel would one day use as ammunition; and Edmund Blackstone. Blackstone! The second reason for Birnie's gloom. But at least his men had been inside the tavern, instead of lounging like mouchers outside.

Ruthven stumbled against one of the patrol, who staggered and tripped over Blackstone's outstretched leg. Birnie almost smiled, took a hold of himself and returned to his desk to await the arrival of Blackstone. Blackstone, the rogue elephant from the herds of St Giles, who was capable of bringing glory and disgrace to the Runners in equal measure; the one Runner whose motives had always perplexed Birnie, the honest Scot.

A thump on the door.

'Come in.' With the stem of his pipe Birnie directed Blackstone to the chair on the other side of his leather-topped desk.

Birnie said: 'I've read your request and it's preposterous.'

'Why's that, sir?' Blackstone inhaled some smuts from the fire and coughed.

'Because, sir, we are custodians of the law, not treasure hunters.'

Blackstone took some snuff to combat the smuts. 'I should have thought', he said mildly, 'that the Runners would be covered in glory if they found Captain Kidd's treasure.'

'Captain Kidd's treasure!' Birnie held his pipe like a gun. 'Are you entering your second childhood, Blackstone?'

'On the contrary, sir, I thought that document' – pointing at his written request – 'was remarkably adult.'

Birnie picked up the request and scanned it, pausing over the penultimate paragraph.

I have today located the said Capt. Maudling in the Trafalgar Tavern at Greenwich. He was at first reticent as to the source of the ruby. Birnie glanced over the top of the document at the big man, too immaculate by far, sitting opposite him and guessed how the reticence had been overcome. *But I finally persuaded him to part with the information. It seems that he was given the ruby in New York, in payment of a debt, by a man named Marryatt. Marryatt, a man of low and venal character,* – Birnie winced – *hinted that he had access to a veritable hoard of valuables.*

Birnie flung the document on his desk. 'How, incidentally, did you find "the said Capt. Maudling"?'

Blackstone stared him straight in the eyes. 'By dint of exhaustive inquiries, sir.'

'You don't expect me to take this request seriously?'

'On the contrary, sir, that's why I stayed up till three this morning penning it. And, as I have pointed out in the second paragraph, I think I am entitled to some leave of absence.' Blackstone flicked a smut off the fine, soft leather of his boots. 'Although I have had second thoughts about undertaking the mission in a private capacity.'

'Really? You mean this should be an official Bow Street inquiry? I'm touched, Blackstone, that you should put the interests of your employers before your own self-indulgence.'

Blackstone took it in his stride. 'As you are no doubt aware, sir, the Government took the existence of Kidd's treasure seriously enough to mount a search at the beginning of the last century.'

Birnie, who didn't know any such thing, said: 'I cannot imagine Sir Robert Peel giving his blessing to any such undertaking.'

'I wasn't aware that the Runners had to have Sir Robert's blessing—'

Birnie snapped: 'You go too far, Blackstone.'

'I'm sorry, sir. But it occurred to me that others in higher office might be interested.'

'Higher than Peel? You mean the Prime Minister?'

Blackstone shook his head. 'I mean the King, sir. As you know, I have recently been employed as his bodyguard at St James's. Prinny – I mean the King – has the rank but not the riches of his position. As he is somewhat fond of the good things of life, it occurred to me that he might give his royal blessing to a mission that could provide him with untold wealth ... '

'King George', Birnie said wearily, 'is admittedly something of a hedonist. But he is not a fool and he wouldn't give his assent to a fool's errand.'

Blackstone proceeded cautiously. 'I took the precaution of calling at St James's on my way here this morning. I saw Sir William Knighton and put my proposition to him. He immediately sought an audience with the King—'

'And?' Birnie, the one-time saddle-maker forever awed by title, looked grimly at Blackstone.

Blackstone stared fixedly at a portrait of Henry Fielding, who had spawned the Runners, and said: 'It seems that the King is more than enthusiastic about the project.'

Birnie sighed. 'So you went over my head, eh, Blackstone?'

'Allegiance to the Crown, sir. I merely implemented it and saved you the trouble.'

'Supposing I forbade this venture?'

'Then, of course, I would abide by your ruling.'

'That's very gratifying to hear,' murmured Birnie, wondering if Blackstone lied as convincingly in court. He picked up another letter lying on his desk. 'By an extraordinary coincidence' – could Blackstone have had anything to do with it? – 'I yesterday received a letter from New York. From the chief police officer there.'

Blackstone looked surprised and Birnie concluded that the surprise was genuine, as far as you could conclude anything with Edmund Blackstone.

'It is a request for your presence in the, ah, New World. The police officer, a man named Jacob Hays, is worried about the increase in crime in his city, apparently a legacy of the immigration after the 1812–15 war. The fame of the Bow Street Runners has reached him. And apparently your *fame*... notoriety... call it what you will, has also reached him,' Birnie said. 'He wants to model his police force on us and seeks your advice.'

'I'm honoured,' Blackstone said.

'It is indeed an honour,' Birnie remarked, deciding that it was also a means to convert abject defeat into a semblance of authority. 'I shall consider whether or not to agree to his request.'

'That's very good of you, sir.'

'Then, of course, any madcap inquiries about Captain Kidd's treasure would be purely incidental.'

Blackstone grinned. 'Unless, of course, I found the treasure. Wouldn't it be official business then, Sir Richard?'

Birnie ignored him. 'Now to more practical matters,' said Birnie, recalling Blackstone's dislike of guard duties. 'You've heard of the Sandwich Islands?'

Blackstone said: 'I read that the King and Queen are visiting this country.'

'Exactly,' Birnie said. 'And you will be guarding them. They're staying at Osborn's Hotel in the Adelphi,' Birnie added, settling back in his chair and appreciating the spring sunshine for the first time that morning. Such warmth, such colour – like gold. 'But book your passage to New York first,' Birnie murmured.

The retired treasure hunter owned a small tavern at Wapping, near Execution Dock. From where he stood, behind the copper-topped bar, the two Bow Street Runners looked formidable.

He said unhappily: 'What can I do for you two gentlemen?'

Ruthven leaned his bulk against the bar and asked for two tankards of ale and two dog's noses.

Blackstone said: 'And some information about buried treasure, Toddy.'

Daniel Todhunter looked perplexed. 'What treasure, Blackie?' He was an unlikely seeker of gold and precious stones; a small man, with a boozer's flush, who apologised obsessively.

'You know what treasure,' Blackstone told him indulgently, sipping his spiced gin and hot water. 'The loot you've dug up over the years.'

Ruthven, uncharacteristically morose, said: 'Want us to turn over the cellars, Toddy?'

'I'm sorry, gentlemen, I don't...'

Blackstone said: 'Don't worry, Toddy, we're not after a percentage.' Our *rightful* percentage as Bow Street Runners, he implied. 'I just want some information.' He told Todhunter about his mission, without mentioning the ruby.

Todhunter apologised for the paucity of his information. 'But, of course, Kidd and treasure are synonymous,' he remarked.

Ruthven, suspicious of words with more than three syllables, frowned.

Todhunter told them that, according to legend, Kidd had buried his loot everywhere on the east coast of North America from Florida to Maine, not to mention the China Seas, the West Indies and the South Pacific. There was much superstition about Kidd's treasure and all piratical loot. Todhunter apologised for mankind's whimsy.

'What sort of superstition?' Blackstone asked, pointing at his empty tankard.

'Sorry, Blackie,' Todhunter said, refilling the tankard. 'Well, you know, tales that a body is buried with every trove and the treasure becomes the property of the Devil. I've got some papers about it if you're interested.'

Blackstone said they were and Todhunter disappeared into the parlour behind the bar.

Ruthven said gloomily: 'So you're leaving us for a pot of gold, eh, Blackie?' He stared at his scarred fists. 'And you know one of the jobs they've already put me down for? Byron's funeral. I never was much of a one for poetry...'

Blackstone stared through the window at the mudflats of the Thames where, in the moonlight, toshermen and mud-larks were searching for coins, intact or rolled into nuggets, in the sewers and underground streams of London. Not the sort of treasure that would have attracted Captain William Kidd, but in London in the 1820s a sovereign gleaming in the mud could keep a family from starving for a month.

Todhunter returned with a copy of an article published in the *Herald of Freedom and the Federal Advertiser* in Boston in 1788, and handed it to Blackstone. It was entitled 'The Art of Digging Money' and recounted tales of the ghosts of pirates, of Deer Isle and of fearful apparitions haunting the sites of buried treasure on the Bluff of Nantasket.

The article discounted these stories and recalled an odd club that had been formed by a group of old women to col-late the tales of the supernatural and exhort their menfolk to lay the ghosts and unearth the loot. They didn't meet with much success and passed their beliefs on to their heirs. The result – in 1788 – was the Deer Isle Money Digging

Society, which had its own peculiar set of rules. Meetings to commence at seven minutes past seven, elections to be held at 7 a.m. on 7 March, the rules drawn up on 7 March 1770 at seven seconds before 7 a.m. ...

'Why?' Blackstone asked.

Todhunter extended his hands in supplication. 'Don't ask me, Blackie. There's so much superstition ... '

'But what about Kidd?' Ruthven asked. 'Where do *you* reckon he hid his cache?'

'Wish I knew, 'Todhunter told him. 'Gardiner's Island off New York, according to some. Recovered in 1699, so the story goes. Who knows? Kidd was in Anguilla when he heard that he was being hunted as a pirate. After that he stopped at the Virgin Islands – where they wouldn't let him set foot on shore – then Mona Island, then north to Lewes in Delaware Bay, then Oyster Bay on Long Island Sound, then Narragansett Bay, then Gardiner's Island, then Boston where he was seized on 6 July 1699. So you see it could be in a hundred and one places ... '

Outside on the mudflats the waifs and sewermen moved in the moonlight like restless ghosts.

'And you never laid a finger on any of it?' Blackstone asked.

'Not as far as I know, Blackie. I found a few coins from time to time in my travels, but nothing that you could put down to Kidd. Nothing that you could tally with this list,' he said, producing the same inventory from the *Quedah* that Fogarty had shown Blackstone.

'But you must have a theory. Every treasure hunter has a theory about Kidd's loot.'

Todhunter looked sly, or perhaps it was the candlelight distorting the incurable lust of a man with the smell of gold in his nostrils. I mustn't become obsessed, Blackstone thought, gazing at the silver pennies of moonlight glinting on the Thames. Todhunter said: 'I'm sorry, Blackie...'

Ruthven leaned over the bar, grasped Todhunter by the lapels of his black, clerical jacket and lifted him up. 'Just a theory, Toddy, that's all we're after.' He held him aloft with ease and waited.

'Well,' said Todhunter, 'if I was still in the business and had the money to sail to America, I'd go looking on Deer Isle in Penobscot Bay.'

Ruthven put him down. 'You're quite a decent fellow, really, Toddy. Now pour us another drink, there's a good lad.'

Blackstone pointed at Todhunter's bundle of papers. 'Mind if I borrow those, Toddy?'

'Of course not, Blackie,' Todhunter said, because he had no choice.

Blackstone gathered up the papers. 'Then we'd best be off. Thanks for your help, Toddy.'

'Think nothing of it,' the tavern-keeper said. 'I'm just sorry I couldn't do more.'

Outside the tavern Blackstone lingered by the gibbet where, on 23 May 1701, Captain Kidd had been hanged – twice.

On the first occasion the rope broke, to the delight of the crowd. Kidd was helped up the scaffold again for the second, successful, attempt. Then his body was hanged in chains at Tilbury Point on the Thames, and swung there for years.

For a moment it was Blackstone standing there on Execution Dock. For a moment it was Blackstone on trial at the Old Bailey, unable to produce the documents that might have freed him, already guilty in the eyes of parliament, proclaiming: 'My lord, it is a very hard sentence. For my part, I am the innocentest person of them all.'

Blackstone shook himself and smiled apologetically at Ruthven, who was as fanciful as a Thames barge. 'Come on,' he said, 'let's get back to the Brown Bear,' thinking of the girl who waited for him there.

He loosened the cravat at his neck because it felt tight, as tight as a hangman's noose.

CHAPTER THREE

He was naked when he first met her. Being sick into a metal washbasin screwed to a table, while a force eight gale raged outside.

As she entered the cabin he grabbed a towel and held it round his waist.

'You must be the famous Blackstone,' she said, looking at him with amusement.

'I am,' Blackstone told her. 'And who the devil are you?' He realised that she was extremely attractive, but he couldn't appreciate it, not with his stomach muscles heaving and the sight of the grey belly of a wave outside the porthole.

'My name's Fanny Campbell,' she said, and Blackstone said: 'I'm pleased to meet you, but I must continue being sick, if you don't mind.'

He bent over the basin again, one hand grasping the towel. The ship rolled violently and two chairs slid across the floor.

'This *is* my cabin,' the girl said.

In the centre of another wave Blackstone thought he saw a fish. He shuddered. He wondered if he should ask the girl to get the Manton pistol from under his pillow and shoot him through the head.

He said: 'I should be extremely grateful if you would leave me alone.'

'Apples,' she said. 'You should have eaten green apples.'

Blackstone groaned and bent over the basin again.

'But don't worry, there's calm weather ahead.'

Blackstone said: 'Madam, if you don't leave I shall drop this towel.'

'Don't let me stop you.'

Blackstone looked up in surprise. She was tall and blonde, with pale skin, and she wore an expensive, low-cut silk dress which enhanced her firm breasts. Blackstone thought she looked Scandinavian; there was also an arrogance about her that, in other circumstances, he would have enjoyed humbling. Now she was laughing at him.

She sat down in a chair that was bolted to the floor and surveyed him as though he was a music hall act.

Blackstone, who had been vomiting on and off for two weeks, said: 'For pity's sake, have mercy. Leave me alone.'

She crossed her legs. 'I don't think you heard me. This is *my* cabin.'

Blackstone glanced around. The door of the wardrobe had swung open, revealing a row of dresses. He groaned. 'I'm sorry...'

During a lull in the storm he had put on some clothes and staggered on deck. But immediately the waves had hurled themselves against the frigate again and he had returned below. To the wrong cabin.

'I believe your cabin is across the passage.' She stood up, walked across the cabin and opened a carpet bag. She took out a brown bottle marked 'Robinson's Sea-Sick Cure' and handed it to him. 'Here, try this. I thought I might need it but, of course, I don't.'

'Of course?' Blackstone swigged from the bottle and grimaced, conscious that whatever he did revealed weakness.

The medicine burned his stomach; he wondered if she'd poisoned him; he didn't care.

She said: 'You look healthy enough. Some interesting scars there, too.'

Blackstone felt like a bull on auction at a fat-stock show. The burning in his stomach was fading; he felt marginally better.

The girl opened a wall cabinet, took out a bottle of cognac and poured herself a glass without spilling a drop. She drank it in a single draught. 'I always like a brandy after lunch,' she informed him.

At the mention of lunch Blackstone decided that he was less than marginally better. He had only appeared for lunch twice since the frigate had left Portsmouth. He devoutly wished he was still at Osborn's Hotel, guarding King Rhio Rhio of the Sandwich Islands and his elephantine Queen Kamehameha. He also wished Captain Kidd had been executed before he had found time to jettison any of his plundered wealth.

He swallowed and gazed out of the porthole. The waves seemed smaller and they had lost their white caps. He vomited a measure of Robinson's Sea-Sick Cure and asked her to pass him the brandy bottle.

The cognac dropped like molten lead into his stomach. He closed his eyes and held on to it. Then he poured some more down his throat in the vague hope that it would choke him.

She looked on approvingly. 'How did you get those scars?'

'I was raped,' Blackstone said, swallowing some more brandy, now unsure whether he was in the last throes of sea-sickness or just plain drunk or both.

'There's no such thing,' she said.

Blackstone choked.

When he had recovered she said: 'Rape is merely the name given to an act to which a certain type of woman submits after a token show of violence. That type of woman is either one who subconsciously enjoys violence or one who has been immersed in the hypocrisy that women should not enjoy making love.'

'I see.' Blackstone decided that he was in the presence of an interesting woman, a woman for whom his fascination would increase as the sensation that an octopus was loose in his abdomen decreased.

'That doesn't mean to say that a woman should submit' – she corrected herself – 'participate in the act if she doesn't like the man concerned.'

'But if he persists, then surely it must be rape.'

The girl smiled at him, a teacher correcting a backward child. 'Rape is impossible.'

'Ah.' Blackstone took another swig of brandy; the movements of the octopus grew feebler. 'I didn't know that.'

'Any woman can prevent rape if she so wishes.'

'Ah.'

The sea was calmer and there were blue sailors' shirts among the scudding clouds. Fanny Campbell had been right about the calm following the storm, she had brought him brandy which was nailing the monster within – he forgave her for the Robinson's Sea-Sick Cure – and she had interesting theories about rape. Blackstone tightened the towel about his waist and sat down opposite her.

Fanny said: 'You see, I believe in free love, the equality of the sexes... It's high time the myth about domination by the male in modern society was sent packing. Can you give me any good reason why man should dominate? A woman produces children, cares for the home, has sensibilities that few men possess...' – a penetrating glance at Blackstone in his towel – 'and is sought after by men. In fact,' she said, taking the cognac bottle from Blackstone, 'there wouldn't be any mankind if it wasn't for women.'

Blackstone, who had decided that brief domination by Fanny Campbell wouldn't be disagreeable, said: 'I think man played some part in it too.' He smiled for the first time since the frigate had left England.

'Merely the instrument of procreation, not its womb.'

'Ah.'

'Woman merely uses man.'

'But you did mention love... free love?'

'A figure of speech.' She tilted the bottle to her lips.

'But why', he asked, wondering why more landlubbers hadn't chanced upon brandy as the universal remedy for sea-sickness, 'are you going to America? Do you imagine that the people there are more...' he searched for the right word, but it was too elusive '...happy with your ideas?'

'Do you think only men should travel?'

Blackstone shrugged.

'I'm going because my father's a friend of a friend of the father of the captain of this ship. Because a woman is just as entitled to search for adventure as a man. And because in England no one appreciates my ideas. I'm ahead of my time.'

She had put the bottle of brandy on the table between them and they both reached for it at the same time. Blackstone allowed her to take it because, he assured himself, he had learnt manners since leaving the Rookery and not because he acknowledged a superior species.

She drank from the bottle and handed it to him, wiping the neck of the bottle and reminding him of George Ruthven's table habits.

Outside the sun appeared and the sea turned from grey to green to burnished steel. Could he make dinner tonight? His stomach responded in the negative. But what a girl. A viking. He imagined her as the masthead of a ship, breasts jutting, flaxen hair streaming.

She said: 'I'm also going up in a balloon.'

'I beg your pardon.'

'A balloon,' she said. 'I 'm going up in one.'

Shortly before Blackstone left England a balloon had ascended from the Eagle Tavern in the City Road. But, at a great height, the gas had been allowed to escape too quickly and the balloon had descended abruptly into the grounds of a certain Lady Gee. He had read a newspaper account of the incident in which the fate of the occupants had been briefly described. *Mr Harris was a corpse and Miss Stocks, aged 18, was on the point of death. But she was taken to the Plough Inn, Beddington, where she recovered.* Blackstone also remembered that another woman, a Miss Fanny Campbell, had been forcibly prevented from ascending, for her own safety. George Ruthven had prevented her and he could imagine how badly she must have taken forcible restraint applied by Ruthven.

He said: 'Now I place you.'

'Ballooning', she said simply, 'is the travel of the future. Women must take their place in the sky with men.'

'You're absolutely right,' Blackstone said, hoping that she didn't know he was a friend of Ruthven. 'I think I would prefer the sky to the sea.'

'And now', she said, 'you'd better be getting back to your cabin.'

'Must I?'

'You must.'

'Ah well.' Blackstone stood up and the towel fell down.

But it was another three days before Blackstone found the courage to participate in the social life of the frigate. He took his place for breakfast at the captain's table, opposite Miss Fanny Campbell, and fought a brief engagement with a boiled egg and some dry toast. Then he went on deck.

The sea was polished and the sky milky fresh and you could sense the depth of the ocean. The frigate seemed a tiny model on a great lake. Although the sea was calm and there was only a puff of wind in the sails, Blackstone still lurched around the deck, watched with controlled amusement by His Majesty's sailors.

Blackstone rolled to the prow of the frigate and stared at the horizon hazed with gathering heat. Ahead lay the New World that had wrested its independence from the British only to fight another war in 1812 when the British fired the city of Washington. How fresh was that memory in the Americans' minds, Blackstone wondered. How would the people of Manhattan, the heart of New York, treat the crew and passengers of a man-o'-war that had, a little over a decade ago, blockaded their city? Blackstone had heard that enmity was dead, that the young nation was too preoccupied with its own emergence to harbour rancour. A fine generalisation which Blackstone didn't doubt, but he also knew that private hatred among the bereaved or maimed survived such generalisations.

Excitement stirred in his breast. In between bouts of vomiting he had been reading about New York, and its contradictions intrigued him. The school books said Henry Hudson had founded it; the Spaniards claimed Gomez; the Italians insisted that it was Verrazano's discovery. If it was Hudson it was an Englishman sailing a Dutch boat; if it was Gomez it was a Portuguese sailing a Spanish boat; if it was Verrazano it was an Italian in a French ship.

In Blackstone's view it was the Indians that had founded it. And subsequently sold the island of Manhattan to the Dutch for the equivalent of twenty-four dollars in beads and ribbons.

And why *Manhattan?* Again the contradictions. *Manahhatin* in Mohican; *Manahachtanienk,* Delaware for 'the place where we all got drunk' (with Henry Hudson)...Blackstone preferred the second of the several theories.

On 6 September 1664 the city, New Amsterdam, was still Dutch; by noon of that day it was British – and subsequently christened New York. Now it was American, a cauldron in which the blood of so many nations bubbled. Once ruled by the peg-legged Petrus Stuyvesant, and built by Peter Minuit, a Huguenot employed by the West India Company!

Blackstone grinned into the barely perceptible breeze. You couldn't avoid meeting adventure in such a city. He glanced at the masts of the frigate. Where was the skull and cross-bones?

At the captain's table that night sat Fanny Campbell and three mere males – Blackstone, a young lieutenant named Forsythe, and the captain himself, a sleek-haired, beardless mariner who had bought his commission. He commanded the ship, but he was obedient to Fanny Campbell.

They drank soup and ate salt beef and leathery Cheddar cheese, washed down with claret.

For the first time since leaving England, Blackstone ate heartily. He was a landlubber and glad of it, and he amused himself through the meal by imagining the captain in the stocks, being pelted with rubbish.

The moon came up and lit a broad avenue on the sea, while the flames of the candles cast small fires on the silver goblets on the table. The gentleness of the night erased some of the arrogance from Fanny Campbell's features.

The captain was recounting some exploit on the China Seas when Fanny Campbell interrupted him: 'For pity's sake, captain, you speak as though your exploits were confined to a man's world.' The captain, who had been telling how he had sunk a Chinese pirate junk with a single ball, looked nonplussed, because if that wasn't a man's world what was? Nonetheless he apologised.

She pressed him. 'I know that such exploits *are* confined to the world of men, but the point is that they shouldn't be. I doubt if there's anything a man can do that a woman can't.'

Blackstone, who could think of one thing, refrained from commenting. He winked at the young lieutenant and applied himself to the claret.

Fanny caught the wink. 'What's so amusing, Mr Blackstone?'

Blackstone spread his hands. 'Nothing in particular.'

'I can guess and it's a typical male attitude. Does sex always have to be a joke?'

'It depends who you have it with,' Blackstone replied. He expected the captain to bark: 'Hold your tongue, sir,' but the captain's only comment was a cautionary clearing of the throat. The young lieutenant coughed into his handkerchief.

Blackstone said: 'I wouldn't have raised the subject, but such bold statements have to be answered.'

'I think Miss Campbell has a point,' the captain replied. 'We do tend to regard ... ah ... *it* as a joke.'

They toasted the King. Blackstone, wearing a royal blue jacket and white ruff, raised his goblet to Fanny Campbell, who was dressed in green silk, the candlelight throwing a shadow on the valley of her bosom.

The men lit cigars and the port was passed round. Fanny showed no sign of retiring; Blackstone suspected she would have enjoyed a puff of his cigar, or a pinch of snuff. Perhaps one day women would achieve equality, and why not? They could do with one or two at Bow Street! Perhaps one day there would be women politicians, a woman prime minister even. Blackstone sipped his port, drew on his cigar and blew grey smoke into the flame of a candle. But it wouldn't be in his lifetime. A pity, because, in his book, a woman was more than a chattel. Especially a beautiful woman.

The lieutenant spoke. 'What chance do we stand in the race, sir?' he asked, addressing the captain, who looked as much like a mariner as a dandy at the Court of St James.

The captain stroked his hairless chin and said: 'We'll lick the Yankees, have no fear,' instantly aligning Blackstone on the side of the American oarsmen who would be rowing against a team from the frigate when they reached New York.

Blackstone said to Fanny Campbell: 'Perhaps we could organise a race against a team of ladies ... '

'Then we'd have our work cut out,' said the captain. He was aged about thirty-five and the port had flowed straight to his cheeks.

'Blow me if we wouldn't,' Blackstone said, grinning at the girl.

The captain said: 'I assume a Runner wouldn't have much experience of sculling, sir?'

'I don't know about that,' Blackstone said. 'I've rowed a few into the dock at Bow Street.'

The lieutenant started to laugh but checked himself when he saw that the captain wasn't amused.

The captain said: 'The Runners have ... ah ... made quite a reputation for themselves, have they not? I hear tell that Peel is none too pleased with their performance.'

'Which Peel would that be?' Blackstone asked.

Fanny said: 'They may be capable Runners, but their sealegs don't seem too steady.'

The captain and the lieutenant laughed uproariously.

Blackstone smiled, puffed at his cigar – and locked Fanny Campbell in the stocks beside the captain.

'That was droll,' the captain said.

'Very droll,' said the lieutenant.

The port went round again. Blackstone turned to Fanny. 'Why did you say you were on board a frigate of His Majesty's Navy?'

The captain answered for her. 'She approached a great friend of my father's and asked if I might provide her with a berth to New York.'

Fanny said: 'And that friend, Mr Blackstone, is Sir Robert Peel, the gentleman whose Christian name you had trouble remembering.'

Blackstone left them in the stocks and took himself to the gallows.

'But of course, my dear,' the captain said, 'Mr Blackstone has a letter from the King himself requesting me to give him a passage to the New World.'

'Ordering,' Blackstone said.

'I beg your pardon.'

'It doesn't matter.' Blackstone stood up, bowing to the girl. 'If you'll excuse me, ma'am, I think I'll take a stroll on deck.'

'Of course, Mr Blackstone.'

On deck Blackstone reflected that, so far, the journey had been one of the most unpleasant experiences of his life. Worse, even, than the time when he had laboured as a navvy on the Stockton and Darlington Railway.*

---

* See *Beau Blackstone*.

After weeks of bilious misery he had recovered only to slight Peel in the presence of the son of one of the Home Secretary's friends. A letter from the King was impressive, but the King wasn't the power in the land. And if the girl was staying in New York, then it was a fair wager that a report of his activities would reach Peel; and his activities weren't going to be confined to advising a police chief.

Seeking solace, Blackstone let the warm night embrace him. The avenue of moonlight led to the stars, soft and close, and, in her wake, the ship left ripples of light. Once again, listening to the flap of the sails, Blackstone began to relax.

To hell with the captain, to hell with Peel. He tossed the glowing stub of his cigar into the ocean. He was on his way to New York, where Captain William Kidd from Greenock, Scotland, had once lived at 56 Wall Street. He was stepping into the shoes of a dead pirate who had been the scourge of the seas. Why should he worry about petty irritations?

He decided to go below.

Blackstone paused outside his cabin. He had made a mistake once and didn't want to repeat it.

Then he heard a cry. And the sound of a scuffle. He hesitated, then knocked on the door of the cabin opposite his. A muffled thud.

'Are you all right?'

He knocked again.

Silence.

Blackstone frowned. One girl among a crew deprived of home comforts since they had left Portsmouth. Equality of the sexes, rape an impossible act...

Another cry, the sound of a struggle.

Blackstone burst into the cabin.

Fanny Campbell was locked in battle with the captain, who had clamped one hand over her mouth. Her dress was torn and one breast was bared.

Blackstone gripped the captain by the arm and pulled him off the girl. The captain swung round, presenting an irresistible target – an open-mouthed face flushed with port and lust.

Blackstone hit him once on the point of the jaw. The captain fell back, cracked his head on the wall and subsided on the bunk.

Blackstone said: 'We Runners have quite a reputation!'

The captain felt his jaw. 'You'll pay for this,' he said, in a voice that suggested his throat was filled with teeth.

Blackstone sucked his fist. 'Willingly,' he said. 'How much?' He turned to the girl. 'Are you all right?'

'Of course I'm all right.' She covered her breast. 'And what right have you to come bursting into my cabin?'

Blackstone, accustomed to most vagaries of human behaviour, stared at her. 'What right?'

'That's what I said. What right?'

'But—'

'I was perfectly capable of taking care of myself.'

'With the greatest respect—'

'I told you rape is impossible.'

'He looked as if he was making a reasonable attempt…'

'Did he?' She had been holding one hand behind her back; now she brought it forward. In her fist she held a pair of scissors.

'Good night,' Blackstone said. 'Sweet dreams.'

He closed the door and went to bed.

CHAPTER FOUR

The balloon hung high in the blue sky.
Blackstone shaded his eyes and watched it carrying its two passengers up the Hudson. It was exciting enough, but it was a distraction on this his first day in Manhattan, with new impressions flitting before him like the swiftly-turned pages of a picture book.

De Vries pointed at the balloon. 'More work for us when it comes down,' he said. 'As if gaslight wasn't enough, we've got balloon fever.'

De Vries, assistant to the High Constable, was a square-shouldered, square-faced man who pondered jokes before laughing at them. He was inclined to be puritanical and, despite the heat, was dressed in a frock-coat and tall black hat. He was descended from the early settlers and was as tough as old Stuyvesant's wooden leg.

They were walking towards the Battery and Castle Garden after a brief tour of the toe of Manhattan. Already Blackstone felt at home. New York had all the vitality of London, much of its elegance and less of its squalor. It was a London with the Thames flooding to faraway horizons, its waters scattered with packet boats with bright, striped hulls and ribbons in their sails, barges, pilot boats, schooners, majestic clippers and those gaudy upstarts, the steamboats.

De Vries had so far shown him Broadway from the Bowling Green, not unlike the curve of Bow Street, with carriages waiting outside elegant terraces, dandies in fine feathers and pale ladies beneath the petals of their parasols; the Stock Exchange, founded by twenty-four brokers who met under a buttonwood tree; the Federal Hall on the corner of Nassau and Wall – built by Lord Bellomont, the man who snared Captain Kidd; the big store A. T. Stewart's with a 'sacrifice sale' in progress; and Brooks Brothers on St Catherine, opposite the fish-market, where Blackstone intended to replenish his wardrobe.

But Blackstone knew that, like London, this city, tiny by comparison, had sores beneath its laundered bandages. And because he had been spawned in just such a sore, he wanted to see Manhattan's afflictions. He also knew that de Vries, a man with a statistical mind, was not the guide to show them to him: de Vries favoured the kind of tour that impressed visitors. De Vries, he decided, was something of a snob.

Which was why they had gone in de Vries's carriage to 223 Broadway, the home of John Jacob Astor, New York's man of property.

'A millionaire,' breathed de Vries. 'Sailed from Germany with two dollars in his pocket. When he was seventeen he made three resolutions – to be honest, to be industrious and not to gamble.'

Blackstone thought de Vries's hero sounded a dull fellow. 'How did he make his blunt?' he asked the Dutchman.

'Blunt?'

'Money.'

'Fur trading to start with,' de Vries said. 'Then property. You know, buying ahead of development. In 1810 he sold property near Wall Street for eight thousand dollars

and purchased eighty lots near Canal Street which became worth eighty thousand dollars. But there are rumours...'
He hesitated.

'Go on,' urged Blackstone, who had spent his professional life on the scent of rumours.

'No, it doesn't matter. Just scandal-mongering.'

They had alighted from the carriage, heading for the Battery. Past neat houses with covered porches and seats on either side, past a couple of wild hogs snouting at them warily.

Blackstone pointed at the pigs. 'Much trouble with them?'

'A little,' de Vries said, diverting attention from the hogs by informing Blackstone that there were now more than five hundred merchants in New York, twelve banks and thirteen marine insurance companies – for a population of 150,000.

High in the hot sky the balloon, now the size of a toy, beckoned them. Sweat streamed down Blackstone's body and he removed his swallow-tail coat. De Vries frowned.

They reached the Battery, where Blackstone sensed de Vries felt at home again because it was patently the place to be. Here was the elegantly-appointed prow of New York's history; ornamental trees and promenades; the rich and the fashionable pressed against the fencing, watching the balloon. No one from the sores of Manhattan here, except perhaps a stray hog or two.

The balloon seemed to be getting larger again.

'It'll be blown out to sea,' said de Vries as the balloon came bowling over the Hudson. 'Come on, let's go into the Garden for a better view.'

They hurried to the Garden, linked to the Battery by a wooden bridge, where once twenty-eight and thirty-eight pounders had guarded the island before Castle Clinton had become Castle Garden. On the terrace, above the coffee house and saloon, they watched the great orange and red balloon sweeping towards them, the two occupants of the basket now clearly visible.

'They'll have to let out the gas,' de Vries said.

'But not too quickly, I hope,' said Blackstone, remembering the fate of the balloonists in England.

'What a crazy game,' the Dutchman said. 'Can you see anything to it, Blackstone?'

'It must be … exhilarating,' Blackstone said. He imagined armadas of balloons roaming the skies, their galleons being plundered by pirates of the air.

The two figures in the basket were working frantically as the balloon swept towards the Atlantic. 'Not too quickly,' Blackstone pleaded. 'Play it calm, lads … '

Suddenly the balloon deflated. It dropped heavily into the river. The crowd was transfixed. Half a dozen small boats started for the balloon, now wallowing like a harpooned whale on the water. Of the basket and its occupants there was no sign.

De Vries and Blackstone stayed for another half an hour, until it was certain that the two balloonists had drowned. Then they returned to Blackstone's hotel, the Eagle on Whitehall and South Street, facing the Battery. When de Vries had left, mourning the stupidity of the balloonists rather than their demise, Blackstone adjourned to Pfaff's beer cellar, concluding over a frothing tankard that Manhattan Island promised to be as exciting as he had anticipated. A fitting base from which to launch a treasure hunt.

First he had to find Marryat, the man who had settled a debt with the American sea captain with a ruby plundered from the *Quedah* by Captain Kidd.

Who better to help him, Blackstone reasoned, than the man who had sent for him, Jacob H. Hays, High Constable of the city of New York?

So that evening, after he had bathed and changed at the Eagle, Blackstone went to call on the police chief, who had been detained at a meeting of the Common Council earlier in the day.

The evening air was warm and heavy. Blackstone wandered along the docks where the bowsprits of tall ships jutted over the quays like bayonets. Girls beckoned from taverns and footpads stalked their prey. Ratcliffe Highway! Unshackled from de Vries, Blackstone had arrived at the sort of scene in which he was at home.

There were lights on the water and songs on the moist air, and the smells of tar and paint filled his nostrils. Behind him a firework exploded over Castle Garden, red and green fires slurred in the dusk.

Blackstone rolled a little as he walked, the Atlantic waves still beneath his feet. And it was the roll, the hallmark of the drunk, that must have attracted the footpad. Instincts finely honed since childhood stirred inside Blackstone.

As the footpad leapt from behind, Blackstone moved swiftly to one side and turned. He dodged the raised cudgel and hit the footpad on his stubbly jaw, jerking him a foot off the ground.

Blackstone picked him up from the cobblestones by the scruff of his moth-eaten blue jersey. He was not a very big footpad and his eyes rolled in fear.

'Lesson number one,' Blackstone informed him. 'Never judge a man by his gait or the cut of his clothes. Or', he added, as the footpad goggled, 'by the way he speaks.'

He picked up the cudgel and tossed it into the water among the dead fish and floating debris. 'Got that?'

The footpad tried to nod.

'Now that's your weapon Right?' he asked, pointing at the hickory club floating in the water.

The footpad gurgled.

'Right. Lesson number two – never be parted from your weapon.' Blackstone heaved his captive into the water next to the cudgel.

Then he dusted himself down, reflecting that the Manhattan criminals had a lot to learn from the English, and was about to go on his way when a girl approached him. A pretty girl wearing gypsy ear-rings, who spoke in twanging broken English.

'That was very clever,' she said, smiling at Blackstone. 'Would you like to buy a girl a drink?' Ratcliffe Highway!

'Why not?' Blackstone said.

They went into a low-raftered tavern where Blackstone bought her a rum and ordered a glass of ale for himself, wondering what form her accomplice would take. 'What's your name?' he asked her. 'And where do you come from?'

'Marie,' she said. 'And I come from up north. From Quebec. And you?'

Blackstone told her.

'I like you,' she said, flinging her arms round him and kissing him. 'If you wait a minute I know of a place where we can go.'

Blackstone grinned at her. 'Fine. But first of all I must tell you that the purse you've just lifted from my pocket belonged to a man dying of the pox.'

She stood back, breathing heavily. Then swore in French and threw the purse on the ground. Blackstone picked it up and put it back in his own pocket. 'Chicken-pox,' he said, finishing his ale, bowing low and walking out into the salty dusk.

It was true, he thought. The police had a crime wave on their hands and they were in sore need of advice. He left the waterfront and headed for the home of the High Constable.

Jacob H. Hays was bald, tough and aggressive. He detested small-time criminals, respected professionals, and fought both relentlessly, armed only with a staff.

He relied largely on night-watchmen – similar to the London Charlies – who reported fire or theft or murder. He also controlled the Watch, a force in which every householder was expected to participate; but many defeated the cause of law and order by paying vagrants to take their place.

Since the end of the 1812–15 war, immigrants had poured into the city which was mushrooming along the old Indian trail, Broadway, spreading across the bouweries, or farms, that Peter Minuit had carved out in the seventeenth century. And with the immigrants came crime.

Hays had heard of the reputation of the Bow Street Runners from seamen who had crossed the Atlantic, and he wanted their help.

After dinner he and Blackstone sat on the stoop drinking coffee. Looking at the big, dark man lounging in front of him, gun in belt, Hays wondered if de Vries had been right in recommending him. He looked more like a villain than a lawman.

He pointed at the Manton pistol. 'Is that necessary?'

'It is where I come from,' Blackstone told him.

'Is it so much worse than Manhattan?'

Blackstone thought about it. 'From my recent experiences' – he had told Hays about the two incidents that evening – 'I would say the London villain is more dangerous because he is more competent.'

Hays shook his head. 'You can't judge our criminals by a couple of river rats.'

'In London the rampsman who attacked me wouldn't have lasted a week.'

'Maybe I'll take you to meet a few of our cracksmen and you'll swallow your words.' Hays rubbed his shining scalp, then grinned suddenly. 'But I didn't bring you all this way to discuss who has the best villains. I want to know how you go about busting them.' He leaned forward. 'I hear you do a bit of detective work.'

'A few tricks like matching a ball with the gun that's fired it.'

'And interrogation?'

'We have our ways,' Blackstone said, enigmatically.

'I've got a client in the cells right now,' Hays said. 'Perhaps you'd like to see how I work?'

'It would be a pleasure,' Blackstone said, taking some snuff and offering the silver box to Hays.

The smells and sounds and sights of Manhattan by night assailed them gently. Across the road at an open window a Dutch woman in pigtails was cooking a meal at a tin-plate stove. From a block or so away came the cry: 'Hot corn! Here's your nice sweet corn all piping hot!' Songs and shouts and the sound of horses' hoofs on cobblestones, all muted in the warm, wet air.

Hays glanced at his gold hunter. 'We'll go down in about half an hour.' He poured more coffee. 'And now, of course, we've got gaslight to add to our worries. But you must have solved that problem in London by now?' He looked inquiringly at Blackstone.

Blackstone sipped his coffee. 'What problem?'

'The gangsters—'

'Gangsters?'

'Villains,' Hays said. 'In the gaslight they can see the mugs – victims – as broad as daylight, turn them over and then disappear into the darkness. What's more, the gaslight makes the horses bolt and there's such a hell of a shindig that it's like taking candy from a baby for the pickpockets. Here, see what the citizens of Manhattan think about gaslight,' Hays said, handing Blackstone a copy of a newspaper.

Blackstone read that the New York Gas Light Company's flaring illuminations were, according to some clergy, 'blasphemous and improving on God's handiwork'; according to some doctors they 'encouraged exposure to the night air'; according to those seeking to ban the sale of alcohol they 'lengthened the hours of drinking'; according to the prudish they 'destroyed the twilight which soothes passion'.

'Looks like it's here to stay,' Blackstone remarked. 'What do you think?'

Hays said: 'If I remember my Bible correctly, "God said, let there be light and there was light".'

Blackstone grinned and stretched. 'Shall we go and see your prisoner?'

Hays stood up. 'He's a hard man. Clubbed one of the watchmen to death for the sake of two dollars, a loaf of bread and a pair of boots.'

'And he admits it?'

'He will,' Hays said, picking up his staff.

The prisoner was German, one of the thousands who had arrived since 1815. He was a giant, with greying hair curling from the neck of his shirt and a shaven head on which stubble was sprouting; he had one good ear and a chewed-up remnant for its fellow. He wore handcuffs which were chained to an iron ring on the wall, but the chain gave him plenty of room to move about and he was sitting at a deal

RICHARD FALKIRK

table eating a hunk of bread and a piece of cheese. When Hays and Blackstone entered he went on eating without looking up.

'Like I told you,' Hays said, 'a tough bastard. That's why we had to chain him up – I reckon he could bend those bars if he wanted to.'

'And you think you can break him?'

'I've broken worse,' Hays answered, bottom lip thrust forward pugnaciously. 'Breaking them has nothing to do with their physical strength. It's up here.' He tapped his gleaming pate. 'But I wish I had some of that sprouting on my scalp,' he added, pointing at the giant's stubble.

The German tore off a piece of bread and stuffed it into his mouth.

Hays asked: 'How would you tackle a thug like this?'

'Is he guilty?'

'Of course. We just need a little more proof.'

'Then I'd hand him over to a friend of mine called George Ruthven.'

'You mean he could beat the hell out of a mean bastard like that?'

'George could beat the hell out of a charging rhinoceros,' Blackstone said.

'And that's all you're going to tell me about your methods of interrogation?'

'There's not much more to tell,' Blackstone said.

'You seem a little reticent.'

Blackstone shrugged.

'Perhaps when we get to know each other a bit better ... ' Hays tapped his formidable nose. 'Or perhaps you've come here to learn from us?'

'Not exactly,' Blackstone told him. 'I hope I'll be able to help you. At least the Runners don't have to guard trees,' he added, referring to a decision of the Common Council to pay twelve dollars to 'J. Hays and five officers attending the Battery at boat race, to protect trees'.

'Don't remind me,' Hays said. 'So how do you think I should proceed?'

'Ask him a few questions first. You can't start beating the living daylights out of a cove before you've given him a chance to talk.'

'Who said anything about beating the living daylights out of anyone?'

'But I thought—'

'You've got a lot to learn, Edmund.'

'Then what are you going to do, bribe him to the gallows?'

Hays shook his head. 'I have perfected my own technique. It usually works perfectly.' He stood in front of the German. 'Well, Müller, have you anything to say?'

The German belched and plugged his mouth with another piece of bread.

'Are you sure he speaks English?' Blackstone asked, looking apologetic as Hays answered abruptly: 'Of course I am.' The police chief cracked his staff across the table and snapped: 'One last chance, did you kill the watchman?'

The German swallowed his bread and spat on the stone-flagged floor.

'You leave me no option ... '

Hays turned to Blackstone. 'You stay here with him. I've got to fetch the means to loosen his tongue.'

When he had gone Blackstone said to the German: 'He's gone to get the thumb-screws. Why don't you tell me what happened and save yourself a lot of pain.'

The German looked at him reflectively, then after a long pause asked: 'You English?'

Blackstone nodded.

'I like English. Good fighters, *ja?*'

'Not bad,' Blackstone conceded.

'I fight an Englishman down the Old Slip. He have my ear.'

Blackstone never discovered what part of the Englishman the German got. They were interrupted by Hays who returned with a jailer carrying a wardrobe.

'Never failed yet,' Hays confided to Blackstone.

They stood the wardrobe upright in front of the German, facing away from Blackstone. Hays opened the door.

The German took one look at its contents and fell face forward on the table. Blackstone took a step forward and peered into the wardrobe, coming face to face with the corpse of the watchman with the side of its head caved in.

Ten minutes later Hays had written a confession and the German had made his mark on it.

'Like I said,' Hays murmured, 'never been known to fail. You must try it yourself when you get back to Bow Street.'

Later Blackstone asked about Marryatt.

'A sneak thief,' said Hays, whose brain was an index of the city's criminals. 'Why do you want to know?'

Blackstone, who had never believed in the unnecessary sharing of information, said: 'I pulled in a gonoph – a sneak thief – in London called Patridge. He said he had family out here, family by the name of Marryatt. He said one of them was a cove called Tom Marryatt. Honest Tom!'

This made Hays laugh. He told Blackstone that Marryatt, sometimes known as Candy because of his love of sweet-meats, followed his trade on the new steamboats that plied the Hudson. 'The girls get on the boats, you know,' Hays explained, 'and Marryatt robs the men with them while they're otherwise engaged.' He chuckled into his glass of Dutch gin.

Blackstone, who had taken a liking to this bald, fearless lawman, contemplated sharing his knowledge with him. Then he thought better of it; he didn't think King George IV of England would take kindly to sharing Captain Kidd's treasure with New York's High Constable. He wouldn't take kindly to sharing it with Edmund Blackstone, come to that, but then he need never know.

They were sitting at a table in a tavern near the Bowery Theatre, where a dancer 'specially imported from Paris' was the star of the show, an import designed to lure patronage from the rival Park Theatre.

'And to think', Hays had said as they entered the tavern, 'that a year ago they were presenting *Othello.'* He didn't say which he preferred.

'Have you had Marryatt in the cells?' Blackstone asked.

'Once or twice. But, you know, he can be very helpful, can Candy Marryatt.'

Blackstone knew.

Hays ordered two more gins. 'Now you say you're not impressed by our villains?'

'Not the ones I've met.'

'Well, we'll see what we can do for you.' He banged his staff on the table and shouted across the crowded, smoke-filled parlour. 'Come and join us Billy.'

An elegant man with hair greying at the temples and diamond rings on his fingers sat down at the table.

'Billy,' Hays said, 'I want you to meet Edmund Blackstone from London town who's come over here to teach us a thing or two about crime prevention.'

'Come to the best man, then,' the elegant stranger said, eyeing Blackstone up and down.

'Best cracksman in the North American continent,' Hays said. 'Aren't you, Billy boy?'

'Mighty kind of you to say so,' said the stranger.

'Tell us about some of your best jobs, Billy, because, you see, Mr Blackstone doesn't think a great deal of the cut of the jib of our villains.'

Blackstone, who realised that he was in the equivalent of Sol's Tavern in London, listened while the stranger, after some encouragement from Hays, recounted how he had bribed a builder constructing a new bank to leave a section of faulty masonry in the wall of the vaults 'from which me and my partners later removed a little gold'.

'Neat,' Blackstone commented. 'Very neat.'

'Banks are my speciality,' the stranger said, modestly. 'They're a challenge.'

'Best cracksman in the business is Billy,' Hays said. 'And see that fellow over there?' He pointed at a lean man with a drooping moustache and a pockmarked face, seated at a table, with a bottle of brandy in front of him. 'Best gun-fighter in these parts, name of Handsom. Which he as sure as hell isn't, 'Hays added.

'You mean you let him roam around free, shooting any-one who disagrees with him?' asked Blackstone, puzzled by Hays' attitude to criminals, which was benevolent even by the Runners' standards.

Hays looked at him in surprise. 'Good God no, not in New York. And Billy, he doesn't crack any safes here, do you Billy?'

The stranger shook his head.

'My job', Hays went on, 'is to control crime in New York. If Billy broke into a bank here, I'd have him inside quicker than you can pull a hair-spring trigger.' He finished his gin. 'No,' he said, gazing with affection at the customers packed into the tavern, 'all the lads here go to work in Boston.'

CHAPTER FIVE

For a while Blackstone relaxed and enjoyed himself on the paddle-steamer ploughing up the Hudson, between banks thick with trees. Flags and ribbons fluttered above the deck; smoke from the twin funnels lingered behind; the paddles churned like treadmills.

Blackstone was enthusiastic about the advent of steam – particularly with the development of railroads in England – but even he found it difficult to associate the movement of the paddles with the plumes of smoke. It was easier to imagine a crew of slaves powering this brightly-painted boat towards Albany.

In a newspaper that morning Blackstone had read about the steamboats, the progeny of Robert Fulton's original vessel, 'precisely like a backwoods sawmill mounted on a scow and set on fire', that had made Albany in thirty-two hours nearly twenty years earlier. According to the paper the steamboats were frequented by women 'of low moral character' and were 'besmirching the fair air with smuts and the pure waters of the Hudson with their slops'.

On deck, in the shade of the canopy, Blackstone observed the 'girls of low moral character', gamblers, card-sharps and pickpockets going about their business. In particular he observed a plump, perspiring man in shirtsleeves who was, in turn, observing the habits of the more prosperous passengers – and eating great quantities of fudge.

Blackstone watched and waited.

The steamboat charged past a sloop-rigged sailing boat with a derisive hoot. The crew of the sailing ship ignored the flamboyant competitor; they would lose the battle, Blackstone thought, but it would be a graceful defeat. As for himself, Blackstone was all for progress: the steamboat was progress and, like most pioneers, it was brash and strong.

Candy Marryatt was watching a red-haired girl with rough cheeks and freckles on the visible curve of her bosom. She was chatting to a middle-aged man with thinning hair and luxurious sidewhiskers who now asked her to sit beside him.

A bottle of champagne was produced and its cork fired into the Hudson. They drank. Candy Marryatt popped more fudge into his mouth, jaws pumping his shiny cheeks.

Below deck there were a few cabins and five rows of triple-tiered bunks which could accommodate five hundred passengers. Blackstone assumed that Sidewhiskers and the red-headed girl were destined for a cabin. He wondered how Marryatt operated: whether he was working with the girl, whether he had duplicates of all the keys, whether the girl would slip a powder into her companion's champagne. It was intriguing, crime in the New World. Perhaps he had been hasty in his first assessment – after all, you didn't find flash cracksmen on London's waterfront.

Blackstone yawned, lulled close to sleep by the heat and the rhythm of the paddles. He took off his waistcoat and laid it on his jacket which was folded beside him. Two little girls in beribboned straw hats chased each other round the seats; ladies fanned themselves energetically; gentlemen snored.

Blackstone closed his eyes, then opened them again with an effort. The scene was unchanged, except that the bottle of champagne was half empty and one little girl had caught the other and was pulling her hair.

Blackstone closed his eyes again and dreamed about Fanny Campbell. They were in a bedchamber in some palatial mansion somewhere in England. Outside a model steamboat chugged across an ornamental lake; inside Fanny was being miserly with her allotments of free love.

Blackstone challenged her. 'Strike me blind, girl, you don't believe in free love any more than I believe in a harlot with a heart of gold.'

She sat on the edge of the bed, unlacing her boots. A well-turned calf, a trim ankle. She laughed at him. 'I believe in free love with a man I like. Now leave my room, pray.' She reached for the bell-pull beside the bed.

Blackstone pulled her arm away. She stood up, one small fist bunched. 'Get out!'

Outside the model steamboat rammed the lakeshore.

Blackstone parried the blow with one arm and, with his free hand, ripped open the front of her dress. Fine bare breasts heaving, a hand clawing at his face ...

He tore off the rest of the gown and threw her on the bed. Then he was beside her, pinioning her arms – as Sir Robert Peel and a squad of red-breasted patrolmen marched into the room.

His head jerked up and a man sitting beside him on the seat eased himself away. They were rounding a fat curve in the river and the sun had found the angle beneath the canopy and was burning the back of Blackstone's neck.

He yawned and stretched and blinked at the dozing passengers. There was no sign of Sidewhiskers, no sign of the red-headed girl, no sign of Candy Marryatt.

Blackstone swore, stood up and headed for the cabins below.

The scene was familiar. The door of the cabin was opening a fraction. Marryatt was taking the wallet that was being pushed through the opening. Blackstone had witnessed similar scenes in many a flash house in London. He assumed that the steamboat was about to make a stop and that Marryatt and the girl would be the first to alight.

He approached the thief from behind, very quietly. Then tapped him on the shoulder. 'Good-day to you, Candy. I think you and me should have a little talk.'

The fat thief jumped and tried to run away. Blackstone held him, fingers digging into the soft flesh beneath his shirt. 'Don't be shy, Candy. You can be of great help to me. You see, I'm writing a book about the techniques of New York's underworld.' He grinned. 'I may even dedicate it to you.'

Marryatt stopped struggling. 'Who the hell are you?'

Blackstone turned him round. 'Doesn't matter who I am, Candy. All that matters is that I've caught you thieving.'

'You English?'

'Astute of you, Candy.'

'How d'you know my name?'

'It doesn't matter.' Blackstone's voice was soothing. 'None of that matters. Now you come along with me.'

Blackstone tried the door of another cabin. It opened and he shoved Marryatt inside, closed the door and pushed the thief on to a chair beside two bunks.

'Now, a few questions.'

Marryatt took a bar of fudge from his pocket and bit into it. Blackstone leaned over and took the wallet from him. It was fat with money.

'Now listen,' Blackstone said, standing in front of Marryatt. 'I want you to answer my questions truthfully. If you don't, then I'll hand you over to the constables.'

A gleam of hope on Marryatt's face. Blackstone said quickly: 'Not New York. Not to Mr Hays. No, I'll hand you over to the lawmen at Albany. I don't imagine they have quite the same working arrangement. And I expect the gentleman who's just been robbed will be eager to press charges...'

'I don't have to say anything to any son-of-a-bitch of an Englishman.'

Blackstone took the fudge from his hand and ground it into the floor with his heel.

'Are you going to be sensible, Candy?'

'What the hell do you want to know?' His voice was as soft as molasses.

'That's better,' Blackstone said. 'That's much better. I'm inquiring about a ruby, Candy.' He watched carefully, noting the fleeting expression of fear.

'What ruby? What the hell are you talking about?'

'You know which ruby. The ruby you gave Captain Maudling in payment of a debt. He told me about it.'

'I don't know what you're talking about.'

Blackstone sighed. 'Don't be stupid. You won't get much fudge in a cell in Albany.'

Marryatt said guardedly: 'Where did you see Maudling?'

'In London. The ruby was stolen from him by another little thief like you. What I want to know, Candy, is where *you* stole it from?'

'I was given it,' Marryatt said.

'Very well, you were given it. Who gave it to you?'

'That's my business.'

'No,' Blackstone said, 'it's *our* business.'

'Why, what's it to you?'

'It has sentimental attachments,' Blackstone said.

'You wouldn't believe me if I told you.'

'I might. Who *gave* it to you?'

'I was given it by a fellow on Broadway.'

Blackstone was puzzled. 'Was he carrying it in his pocket?'

'Not exactly.'

'Where?'

'In a jewel case.'

'And he was carrying the jewel case?'

Marryatt tried to get up and Blackstone pushed him down again.

'Where, Candy?'

'On the dressing-table in his bedroom.'

'Ah, so you got a bit ambitious, eh? Did a spot of house-breaking, did you?'

'I just happened to be in his house.'

'In his bedroom?'

'He told me I could have it.'

They were all the same, Blackstone thought. They were confessing. They knew it and you knew it. But still they had to dress the confession up with implausible lies.

'Very well, so he told you that you could have it and you helped yourself. Very generous, wasn't he? You know, that ruby's worth a fortune.'

Marryatt frowned. 'How much?'

'It doesn't matter. Far more valuable than anything you've ever had in your sticky little fingers.'

'But Maudling told me it was only worth a few dollars.'

'Then Maudling was lying to you. Now, where did you get it from?'

'I told you, this fellow on Broadway.'

'A jeweller?'

Marryatt shook his head. Outside, the paddles were slowing down and Blackstone guessed they were nearing Marryatt's escape exit. Any moment now there would be a commotion when Sidewhiskers discovered his wallet had been pinched and Blackstone didn't want to be in the vicinity when it happened.

'Who, Candy?'

'Fellow with a big house.'

'Who?'

'I don't know who he was. Just a fellow in a big house.'

'But you said he gave you the ruby. You must know who he was.' Blackstone noticed a new kind of fear in Marryatt's manner.

'I don't. Honest.'

Blackstone leaned forward and slapped Marryatt hard across the face. 'Who?'

'He's a businessman. I said you wouldn't believe me ... '

'Try me.'

'Name of Astor,' Marryatt said. 'Jacob Astor.'

Next day Blackstone caught the stagecoach from Albany back to New York.

Exhausted, he went to bed early in the Eagle Hotel, listening to the sounds of the river, the flap of sails and the creak of rope against wood. Just before falling asleep he fancied he was on the banks of the Thames beside Execution Dock – 'My lord, it is a very hard sentence. For my part, I am the innocentest person of them all.'

CHAPTER SIX

First Blackstone had to study his subject. John Jacob Astor, formerly Jacob Ashdour, of Waldorf, Germany, son of a butcher. At the age of seventeen he had left home with the equivalent of two dollars in his pocket and, after working for a time in London, had sailed for America.

Now he was the richest man in North America, the landlord of New York.

To fill in the details Blackstone consulted Astor's confidential adviser, a man named Fitz-Greene Halleck. They met on the Battery on another hot morning, the waters of the bay flat and blue, sails on the ships hanging limp. The Battery was crowded with New York beaux in tall hats and tight trousers, and girls in dresses with leg-o'-mutton sleeves and elaborate bonnets. They were watching a race between two rowing boats.

'You must realise', Halleck said, 'that I am Mr Astor's *confidential adviser.*'

'I know,' Blackstone said, as they strolled beneath the trees. 'That's why I consulted you.'

'Exactly what sort of article do you propose to write for *The Times*?'

'Just a general essay about the personalities of New York.'

'You don't look like a writer,' Halleck said, doubtfully.

'What does a writer look like?'

'There you have me,' Halleck admitted.

Halleck was a cultivated man in his late thirties, financial expert, minor poet and patriot. His forehead was broad, his nose aquiline, his lips thin.

In the 1812–15 war he had been one of the 112 members of the élite Iron Greys, a light infantry company which had once camped on the Battery; but they had never been called upon to fight and their fervour still burned brightly. Halleck was one of the organisers of Evacuation Day, held to commemorate the day in November 1783 when the British departed and George Washington arrived, at the end of the War of American Independence.

Even now, as they walked in peace on the Battery, Blackstone sensed that Halleck was seeing tents with soldiers sprawled outside, waiting for the British who had never attacked.

Blackstone said: 'Of course, I shall cover notabilities in every field of life this century. DeWitt Clinton, Aaron Burr, Fulton, Cornelius Vanderbilt, Samuel Swarthout...'

Halleck smiled. Swarthout, tried for treason with Aaron Burr, had been captain of the Iron Greys. 'Full marks for fieldwork, none for subtlety,' he said. They turned at Castle Garden and retraced their footsteps, behind the crowd which was shouting encouragement to one of the crews of oarsmen. 'What exactly do you want to know?'

Blackstone shrugged. 'Just a little of Mr Astor's background – and your own impression of him, perhaps.'

Halleck described how Astor had clawed his way to riches.

In New York he had worked for a Quaker named Robert Browne, for two dollars a week and board. Browne was in the fur business and Astor had learned a lot from the traders. He was promoted to buying stock in Montreal, where he drove hard bargains with the Indians. Then he started his own business and sailed to London – steerage, Halleck emphasised – where he sold furs at fantastic profits. He also became agent for Astor and Broadwood (his brother and partner) and sold musical instruments.

His first venture into real estate involved the purchase of two lots on Bowery Lane for 625 dollars. 'But in the early days', said Halleck, 'it was fur that brought in the cash. The old China Sea trade. Furs to Canton, then tea back to New York. There were enormous import duties, but he didn't have to pay these for eighteen months – in other words he always had an interest-free loan and he invested his money in property.'

'That was what made him a millionaire. Always buying ahead of development. He bought Richmond Hill, Aaron Burr's estate, for one thousand dollars an acre and sold it twelve years later for fifteen hundred dollars a lot. He bought farms on Bloomingdale Road, John Selmar's East Side Farm, half of Governor Clinton's farm…in fact a good part of Manhattan Island,' Halleck said. 'A strange man, a visionary in a way.'

'In what way?' Blackstone asked, catching a glimpse of the two crews of oarsmen approaching the Battery.

'He's not parochial. He sees America as a vast entity stretching from east to west. He wanted to control the fur trade from the Great Lakes to the Pacific by establishing chains of trading posts—'

Blackstone interrupted the flow of Astor's idealism. 'But there are other theories about his wealth, aren't there?' he asked.

'Ah, so you've heard the rumours too.'

'I've heard a few stories.'

'Well, they're all nonsense.'

'Ah.'

'Pure claptrap.'

'It all sounded a trifle unlikely,' Blackstone murmured.

'The stuff of fantasy,' Halleck said. And then: 'What exactly have you heard?'

Blackstone stared into the hot sky, seeking inspiration. Had de Vries been referring to Captain Kidd's treasure? If not, then Blackstone would be falling into a trap. 'You know, the usual sort of stories,' he said.

Halleck stopped walking. Hands on hips, he turned to Blackstone, laughed and said: 'You don't know a damned thing, do you, Mr Blackstone?' And Blackstone smiled back at him and said no, he didn't.

'You should have been a policeman, sir, not a writer.'

Blackstone laughed loudly.

They sauntered on. Then Halleck said: 'Well, I suppose you might as well know. It's pure gossip and, as I told you, utter nonsense.'

'Then I might as well know,' Blackstone agreed.

Halleck paused. 'You did say *The Times*, Mr Blackstone?'

Blackstone nodded.

'Well, that's all right, then. They wouldn't print rubbish like this. It's so ridiculous it's not even laughable.'

'Then I shan't laugh,' said Blackstone, who guessed that Halleck was playing a game with him. After all, he was English, the enemy which had failed to turn up and engage the Iron Greys.

Halleck relented. 'I shan't keep you in suspense any more, Mr Blackstone. You see, there was a rumour that Astor had access to Captain Kidd's treasure. Have you ever heard of anything more fatuous?'

Never in his life, Blackstone said, had he heard of anything more fatuous.

Further up the Hudson a roar of excitement was gaining volume as the rowing boats approached the Battery.

'Come on,' Halleck said, 'let's go on to the terrace at Castle Garden – I've got a season ticket.'

From the terrace they could see the two boats surging through the water, foam creaming past the bows, oars dipping rhythmically.

The course was four miles, starting and finishing at the Battery, turning at a marker upstream. There was little in it now as the two boats skimmed towards the finish. On the quays hats were flying in the air, children fell into the water and dogs howled with the excitement of it all.

'Do they always get as emotional as this?' Blackstone asked, hand to his eyes.

'Only when we're racing the British,' Halleck told him.

Then Blackstone remembered – the race between four of the frigate's crew and a New York team.

One boat edged ahead.

'Who's winning?' Blackstone asked.

'We are.' The urbane man-about-town snatched off his hat and let out a yell. 'Come on, pull, heave, speed it up lads...'

The frigate's oarsmen were rowing with long graceful strokes; the Americans rowed with stiff backs, digging their oars into the water and pulling them back with a jerk. On this day sinewed grace was the loser.

The American boat accelerated and swept past the finish fifty yards ahead of the British.

Halleck bellowed happily – and so did Blackstone. Halleck looked at him curiously. 'An odd response from an Englishman – a correspondent of the London *Times*...'

'The best team won,' Blackstone explained, imagining the expression on the captain's face.

'Hmmmm.' Halleck eyed Blackstone speculatively. 'Let's go and have some coffee,' he suggested, taking Blackstone's arm. 'I feel quite elated. That was almost as exhilarating as the day the *American Star,* our pride and joy, defeated the *Dart,* the racing boat from your frigate *Hussar,* by three hundred yards. I imagine you would have enjoyed that just as much,' he murmured, shaking his head as they headed for the saloon, where an orchestra was tuning up.

Blackstone, who had decided that an unpatriotic Englishman might arouse suspicion, said: 'It's always a pleasure to see colonials coming into their own.'

Halleck smiled. 'It was the crew of the *American Star* that rowed Lafayette across the Hudson when he went to Philadelphia. But you should have been here the day Lafayette came to New York, years after he fought beside Washington. By then he was an old man of sixty-seven without a dollar to his name. But he received a hero's welcome. And he landed right here,' Halleck said, 'on Castle Garden. Guns fired a major-general's salute and crowds pelted him with flowers through Bowling Green and up Broadway. That's how we got our National Guard,' Halleck added.

'Oh?'

'Some officers of the Eleventh Regiment were talking about forming a new battalion. So they called it the *Garde Nationale,* which Lafayette had commanded in France. Hence the National Guard.'

They sat at a table near the orchestra, which was playing gentle music. Halleck ordered coffee and told Blackstone that he was expecting the company of a young lady – 'a rather unusual young lady who is already causing quite a stir in the fashionable circles of Manhattan'.

But Blackstone was back on the bullion trail. He sipped his coffee and asked casually: 'How on earth did this ... this absurd rumour about Astor begin to circulate?'

'How *do* these rumours start? Jealousy, I should imagine. Enemies who are unable to accept that a man can make a million from trading and speculation.'

'An odd theory, though. Captain Kidd's treasure!'

Halleck dismissed the absurdity with a wave of his hand.

Blackstone said: 'What kind of a man is Astor?'

'I thought I'd told you.'

'No, sir, you didn't. You told me what he had achieved. Now I should like to know the opinion of Fitz-Greene Halleck the poet. You tell me he is a visionary – but a visionary can be exuberant, quiet, cantankerous, benevolent ... '

Halleck's mood seemed to change. He said quietly: 'John Jacob Astor is a careful man.'

Mean in other words, Blackstone concluded.

'A deeply religious man, devoted to his family.'

A Bible-thumping miser!

'But a fair man.'

Which meant he paid a fair wage, which meant he paid his employees just enough to live on.

'With respect,' Blackstone said, 'you don't wax very poetic about him.' He wondered how much Halleck expected to be left in Astor's will.

Halleck stood up. 'Ah, there you are, my dear,' he said. 'Allow me to introduce Mr Blackstone from the same fair city as yourself.'

Blackstone stood up. 'We've already met,' he said to Halleck. 'How are you enjoying New York, Miss Campbell?'

And how am I going to keep you from exposing me as a liar and a fake, he wondered. My only hope is Fanny Campbell's loyalty. But why should she be loyal?

Fanny Campbell said: 'I've been thoroughly enjoying myself—'

But before she had time to finish the sentence Blackstone told her: 'Mr Halleck is helping me with my series of articles for *The Times.*' He awaited the denunciation.

A fleeting expression of puzzlement, which he hoped only he noticed, crossed her face. Then she said: 'Really? That's very kind of you, Mr Halleck. Which particular aspect of Mr Blackstone's... ah... articles are you helping him with?'

'A few facts and figures about Mr Astor,' Halleck said. 'As I told you, I act as his confidential adviser...'

'Ah yes,' she said, 'so you did.'

The orchestra swung into a selection of old English country dances.

Halleck took a silver watch from his waistcoat pocket. 'And now I have a confession to make. I have an urgent business appointment. But I knew Mr Blackstone would be joining me this morning and I hoped' – looking inquiringly at Blackstone – 'that he might be able to entertain you until I return.' He glanced at his watch again as though he hadn't understood it the first time. 'I'll only be an hour. Is that all right with you... Miss Campbell, Mr Blackstone?'

They said it was.

He smiled, stood up, bowed, did all the right things. Blackstone wondered if he was running off to tell John Jacob Astor that a man who looked as much like a representative of *The Times* as a dockside footpad had been asking questions about Captain Kidd's treasure.

Blackstone didn't know what to make of Fanny Campbell. High-class whore? Sexual visionary? Man-hater? Man-lover? A woman scared of her own passions? A woman trying to disguise lack of passion? Whichever way you looked at her, she was formidable.

Blackstone watched her drinking her coffee. Cool and Nordic despite the heat, fair hair in ringlets, low-cut blue dress matching her eyes. Blackstone remembered his dream.

'What are you thinking, Mr Blackstone?'

'This and that,' Blackstone replied.

He had known many women, but this one was unlike any he had met before. And, as he smiled at her, the possibility crossed his mind that perhaps she was genuine, perhaps she did believe in the equality of the sexes. And why not? Why shouldn't women have equal opportunities with men?

She said: 'So we work for *The Times* do we, Mr Blackstone?'

'Blackie,' he said. 'Most people call me Blackie.'

'On *The Times*?'

Blackstone said: 'I was travelling incognito on the ship. You know, if people know you work for a newspaper they dry up.'

'Don't insult my intelligence,' she said.

'I wouldn't dream of it. And I'm most grateful to you for not expressing surprise that I worked for *The Times*.'

She stood up. 'Let's walk Mr … Blackie.'

They strolled along the lower promenade, with its paintings and marble statues representing the four seasons of the year.

'Now,' she said, as they walked past Winter, 'what's this all about?'

'I'm here on a special assignment for the King,' said Blackstone, surprised as always at his ability to marry fact and fiction.

'Really? Why would the King choose a Bow Street Runner to carry out an assignment?' She thought about it. 'It must be a thoroughly disreputable assignment.'

'Thank you,' said Blackstone, with dignity.

'And you don't look much like a representative of *The Times*.'

'No?'

'More like a representative of London's underworld considering expanding into the New World. A criminal with breeding,' she added kindly. 'A cracksman or something like that.'

'Manhattan's ripe for that sort of expansion,' Blackstone said, as they passed from Winter to Spring. 'Now, can I count on your discretion?'

Fanny said: 'You can count on nothing,' and smiled at him.

'I must insist.'

'Really?' She hastened her step. 'You can insist on anything, my dear Blackie. We're not in London now and you can't cart me off to one of your cells on some absurd pretext.'

I could give you a good hiding, Blackstone thought.

'So really,' she went on, 'I've got you where I want you, haven't I, Mr Blackie. Unless of course—'

'I tell you what the assignment is?'

'My', she said, 'but you're quick.'

Ever since childhood, when he had been called upon to explain the presence of gentlemen's silk handkerchieves in his own pocket, Blackstone had been an accomplished liar. Now was the time to muster all his prowess. But was it? Already his New York identity was split three ways – adviser to the police, treasure seeker and *Times* correspondent, the latter being necessary because the reputation of the Runners had reached America and Halleck would have been suspicious. Blackstone decided that yet another lie would drive him out of his mind.

Would it really matter if she divulged his true identity? After all, Hays and de Vries knew, although they would be perplexed at his sudden emergence as a newspaperman. But Halleck would probably start ringing alarm-bells all over the Astor household. No, Miss Campbell, you'd better keep quiet. Eat humble pie, Blackie.

He said: 'I implore you, Miss Campbell, to exercise discretion. The assignment is of the utmost importance to His Majesty and the Government.'

'Don't be so pompous,' said Miss Campbell. 'It's out of character. And what's more, it means you're lying.'

From Spring to Summer. Past an entrance to the saloon, where the orchestra had swung into a polka.

'And furthermore,' Fanny said, 'I can't take a man, even a Bow Street Runner, very seriously when I've seen him being sick in my handbasin wearing only a towel. And without a towel, come to that,' she said reflectively.

Blackstone shrugged. Too much humble pie stuck in his gullet. 'On your head be it. If you don't help me I'll see that you're carted off to the cells immediately you set foot in England.'

'Lor!' she exclaimed. 'And what makes you think I want to return to England?'

Blackstone looked at her in surprise. He assumed everyone wanted to return to England.

'They're too stuffy over there,' she said. 'That's why I came here.'

'Stuffy? In London?'

'Perhaps not in your London. But in mine, certainly.'

'And what are you going to do here that you can't do in London?'

'I'm going to preach free love.'

'Good grief.'

'And I 'm going to go on the stage.'

'And?'

'I've already told you – I'm going up in a balloon.'

'You could have done all that in London.'

'Everything, perhaps, except preach free love.'

As they moved from Summer to Autumn and back to Winter Blackstone wished fervently that she would practise what she preached.

Later, after Halleck had returned, they supped ale in the saloon, Fanny having turned down the offer of coffee, tea, mineral water or even a little Madeira.

After they had been talking for ten minutes or so, Halleck slipped away to chat to a friend at another table. While he was gone Fanny leaned across the table and said: 'I might relent if—'

'If what?'

'If you show me … the other side of Manhattan.'

'What other side?'

'The sort of places a Bow Street Runner would frequent.'

'But surely, Miss Campbell, if you believe in the equality of the sexes, then you should be able to visit those places alone.'

She glared at him.

He grinned. 'Very well. Would tonight suit you?'

She nodded. And, as Halleck returned, she remarked that he should be able to find some colourful material for his articles in *The Times*.

CHAPTER SEVEN

Gas flared in Manhattan. In bright white blossoms that made the night beyond abrupt, spilling counterfeit moonlight on the sidewalks, imparting the pallor of death to the ruddiest of cheeks.

To those citizens who attributed all progress to the devil, gaslight was the illumination of hell – and heaven was still lit by whale-oil lamps and candle-lanterns.

In Castle Garden there was gas, flooding the terraces with ghostly light, transforming flowers into stars.

Gas from the works at Hester and Centre Streets was in the better hotels. *Don't blow it out* – thus ran the warning on bedroom walls. Gas was in the streets and in some of the taverns; gas was reflected in the dark waters that lapped the island of Manhattan.

It was all due to the efforts of Messrs Thomas Morris, Samuel Leggett and Josiah Ogden Hoffman who, on 21 February 1823, had alighted from the Albany stagecoach, seeking a charter for the New York Gas Light Company.

But it was too early for gaslight as Blackstone set out, on a horse loaned to him by de Vries, for the village of Greenwich, where Fanny Campbell was staying with distant relatives of her family. He had suggested a carriage, but no, she had been loaned a horse and she, too, would ride.

He rode past the white doors and green shutters of Bowling Green, the elegant terrace opposite the Green, known as Nobs' Row, then cantered towards the heart of the island flanked by the Hudson and East Rivers, smelling the countryside sweating after the hot day, enjoying the illusion of speed in the dusk, wondering where the hell the Indians were.

After a short ride he reached Greenwich, which was populated by refugees from the 1822 yellow fever epidemic. Fanny was waiting outside a cottage surrounded by sweetbriar bushes; a white horse was tethered to the porch.

Blackstone dismounted to help her into the saddle. But she had mounted before he reached her.

They headed back towards Manhattan Toe, first trotting, then cantering, then galloping. A race.

She reached Bowling Green a hundred yards ahead of him. But it was the horse, not the rider, that won a race. Wasn't it?

'Right,' she said when he caught up with her. 'What devil's kitchen are we visiting first?'

Blackstone, still doubtful, said: 'There are some pretty tough places here. It is a port after all. Perhaps we should just visit Castle Garden—'

'Certainly,' she said, 'if you really want me to tell Halleck that you're a Bow Street Runner.'

'So be it. But don't blame me—'

'No one will blame you. Now, for God's sake, let's go.'

Blackstone took her first to Pfaff's beer cellar, which had prospered since the influx of Germans. They tethered their horses and went inside; a German band – everyone from Germany seemed to be a bandsman, a butcher or an intellectual – clad in leather shorts was playing Bavarian music.

Unsolicited, a waiter put two foaming steins on the table in front of them.

Fanny said: 'We won't stay here long.'

'Whatever you say, ma'am.'

She took a long pull of lager. 'It's a man's world isn't it ... Blackie?'

'Thank God,' he agreed.

'It shouldn't be, you know.'

'Whether you like it or not, man is the breadwinner.'

'While the woman has his children, keeps his house and warms his bed for him. Surely she is just as entitled to a slice of the pie as he is?'

'I think you'll find that most women whose husbands can afford to have servants have a fair slice of the pie.' Blackstone warmed to his subject. 'I think they enjoy the good things of life, while the wet-nurse feeds their children and the dollymop gets swollen knees scrubbing the floors, and then gets dismissed when she can't work any more ...'

'You have a point,' said Fanny, looking at him in surprise. She was wearing a riding habit, her face was flushed and she looked just as Bavarian as the bandleader smacking his leather shorts to the rhythm of the music. 'But surely what you've said proves my argument. Does the coachman or the footman get dismissed? Do they earn a paltry seven pounds a year like your dollymop? Do they get swollen knees from scrubbing floors? And furthermore,' said Fanny, peering at him over her stein, 'I don't accept that the mistress of the house has a fair slice of the pie. Tea-parties, riding in the park, the occasional theatre, gossip, tittle-tattle—'

'Perhaps that's what they want. Not what *you* want, but what they want. Are you so sure you represent the views of other women? What would you have them doing – attending prize-fights? Participating, perhaps ...'

She smiled. 'Why not?' She finished her lager. 'Now let's move on.'

Blackstone sighed.

They left their horses outside Pfaff's and made for Broad Street. The gaslights were flaring now, attracting knots of people like moths – street vendors selling mint from willow baskets and clams from wooden buckets, an Italian organ-grinder and his monkey, children begging, a man with a flowing beard selling ballads, a fire-eater, upright citizens and downright villains...

They wandered around, two foreigners in a strange port, sharing its sights and smells and sounds. Then old instincts of self-preservation that had kept Blackstone alive in the stews of London surfaced: he suspected they were being followed.

He stopped suddenly and glanced round. A movement in the shadows beyond the gaslight? Perhaps. But why not? All of Manhattan seemed to be on the streets this sweltering night: men, women, children, dogs and hogs...

Perhaps I'm becoming too sensitive to danger, he thought, like some people are about their health.

'What's the matter?' she asked.

'I don't know—'

'Not looking for an excuse to cancel the evening, are you?'

'Of course not.' Blackstone took her hand and tucked it under his arm and she didn't resist. 'We might as well look as if we're together,' he said, leading her across a cobbled street.

'Where are we going?'

'To a tavern I know of.'

'Full of ... interesting people?'

'Full of criminals,' Blackstone told her.

He took her to the tavern near the Bowery Theatre which he had visited with Hays.

'Want to meet a cracksman?'

She nodded, ringlets bobbing, and Blackstone took her to the table where Billy the bank-robber was sitting with his cronies. They drank some gin and Billy, diamonds glittering on his fingers, recounted more of his exploits.

Half-way through a tale of how he had spent a week undermining the wall of a bank, while disguised as a nightwatchman, Blackstone excused himself and made for a door at the far end of the parlour. He walked down a passage, let himself out at the rear entrance and made his way along a lane towards the gas-lit street.

At the end of the lane he paused. If he was being followed, then his pursuer would be somewhere near the entrance to the tavern.

He saw two drunks helping each other along the sidewalk, a few swells heading for the theatre, a little girl with shadows pencilled beneath her eyes, singing a plaintive song.

And a man with his back to Blackstone, lurking on the edge of a pool of gaslight.

Blackstone approached quietly.

He tapped the man on the back and said: 'Good evening, captain. Waiting for someone?'

The captain of the frigate swung round. 'What the devil!' There was a bruise on his jaw and one of his teeth was missing.

Blackstone smiled at him and said: 'Bad luck about the race this morning.'

The captain recovered himself. 'What the hell do you want?'

'Nothing. Just passing the time of the evening.'

'I suggest you pass it somewhere else.'

'How can I when you're following me?'

'Following you? Are you out of your mind? Frankly, Blackstone, you're the last person on God's earth I would want to follow, and if you don't get out of my sight I'll call my shore patrol and clap you in irons.'

'Shore patrol? I see no shore patrol.'

'You will', the captain said, jaw-muscles working, 'if you don't get out of my way.'

'Tut tut,' Blackstone said. 'You shouldn't be such a bad loser. I'm referring to the race, of course ... Or were you following Miss Campbell?'

'I wasn't following anyone. You seem to have a mistaken idea of your own importance. Bow Street doesn't mean a damn in Manhattan.'

'I saw you, captain. You've been following us ever since we left Pfaff's.'

'You're out of your mind.'

'I don't think so,' Blackstone said, wondering if he was. 'Why are you standing out here? If you want a drink why don't you go into the tavern? If you want to see the French dancer's ankles why don't you go into the theatre?'

'Mind your own damn business,' the captain said. 'And when you return to London, Blackstone, watch out. Sir Robert Peel shall hear about you.'

'And he will hear *from* me,' Blackstone said. 'Assault on the high seas, captain, is a hanging offence.'

Blackstone turned abruptly and strode back into the tavern, where the bank-robber was recounting how he had sawed through the bars of a bullion vault.

After that the girl insisted on visiting various premises on South Street, which faced the jostling ships on the East River. She drank several gins, holding her liquor better than many men Blackstone knew, and she scared off one seaman who made a grab at her by brandishing a hat-pin.

Beneath a full moon they walked back along South Street, turning right at the Old Slip and reaching Hanover Square unscathed.

'And now,' Blackstone said, 'home to bed.'

'But we've only just started.'

'The evening is concluded,' Blackstone said. 'And if you want to tell Halleck who I am, feel free to do so.'

The horses were still outside Pfaff's.

'But I don't think you should ride back to Greenwich,' Blackstone said, after glancing at his Breguet and discovering to his surprise that it was 3 a.m. and thinking that he was damned if he was going to ride to the village and back again. 'There are plenty of rooms at my hotel.'

She didn't object.

He booked another room from a yawning porter and escorted her upstairs.

She entered the room and he went in with her.

They faced each other. He had rehearsed the moment several times. At the first hint that she was unwilling to share his bed, he would bow, murmur his excuses and withdraw, bolstering his damaged pride.

But the first night was nothing like the rehearsal.

She drew the red satin curtains apart and opened the windows.

Neither of them spoke. Neither suggested nor demurred. They both undressed. The equality of the sexes was preserved.

He led her to the four-poster bed, or she led him. He thought she looked magnificent – fine, rosy-tipped breasts, flat belly and cushion of curls. She thought he looked magnificent – aroused and hard, firmly-muscled and scarred.

And then they were on the bed, wild and uninhibited, and to hell with equality. It had, Blackstone reflected, been a long sea voyage.

With the dawn came a change in her mood. It was often thus – guilt, recrimination, fear.

With her it was caution.

Curtains, Blackstone decided, should always be closed before dawn searched the bedroom.

But he knew what she would say as she lay there in the hesitant light, more vulnerable than she liked to be.

She said: 'I hope you don't think—'

'That I seduced you?' He raised himself on one elbow. 'Of course not. We ... seduced each other.'

'Mmmmmmmmm.'

'And I hope you don't think—'

'That I seduced you?' As the daylight strengthened her aggression returned. 'I rather think I did. After all, it is my room, I did ask you in ... '

'This discussion is ridiculous,' Blackstone said, smoothing flaxen hair from her forehead. 'The woman usually accuses the man of seduction – she doesn't claim the honour for herself.'

'Really? I wouldn't know.' She moved away from him. 'You're a strange man, Blackie. I thought you were all shallows at first, but there are depths there, too. You know, when you were talking about the dollymops last night ... Tell me about yourself, Blackie, tell me about your childhood.'

And, with a lot of prompting, and speaking in halting phrases, Blackstone told her about his early life in the Rookery, his ignorance about the identity of his father, his activities as a child thief, culminating in his capture by an old gentleman who had led him to the other side of the law and to Bow Street.

Blackstone felt vulnerable. 'Now it's your turn,' he said.

And she told him about her disciplined upbringing in a mansion just north of Highgate village, of her puritanical father, a widower, and her sadistic tutor; of an atmosphere in which you were taught to be ashamed of your body; of her flight to the wicked city of London and the disgrace she had enthusiastically brought to her father's name.

And now they were equal again.

Blackstone got out of bed and walked naked to the window. A toy balloon sailed past, heading out to sea. The sun was rising and the sky was hazed with latent heat.

Before returning to the bed Blackstone closed the curtains.

CHAPTER EIGHT

It wasn't the first house Blackstone had broken into.
Many years ago he had been a snakesman, a boy used
by a cracksman to enter a house through a small aperture
and unlock the door. Since then his professional duties had
necessitated his unlawful entry, in the interests of the law,
into a dozen or so dwelling-houses.

The easiest method was to use an accomplice, dollymop, cook, footman or even butler. Blackstone suspected
that this was how Marryatt had got his hands on the ruby,
because he didn't have the air of a burglar. But Blackstone
didn't favour partners – they might blab or blackmail. He
preferred to work alone.

So forced entry into the residence of John Jacob Astor,
away in Philadelphia with his family, had to be a professional screwing job.

Like any cracksman worth his salt, Blackstone had
staked out 223 Broadway, where Astor had lived for twenty-
five years. He had discovered the taproom, where the staff
besported themselves in the absence of the owner; he had
observed the habits of the night-watchman; he had noted
the times the Watch marched past; he had searched for the
weak link in the defences of the fashionable but modestly-
appointed house.

The classic method of entry would have been a blank key: coat it with wax, insert it in the keyhole so that the indentations in the lock are reproduced on the wax, get a new key cut, and in you go as though you owned the place. But that would take time and would mean a locksmith as an accomplice. Blackstone didn't want accomplices.

So the break would have to be crude. Blackstone regretted this. But, he thought, burglars can't be choosers!

He picked out a side door made of wood which didn't look too stout. Then he set about fixing the staff. Blackstone knew a good deal about servants, including the fact that, in their master's absence, their loyalty was often tenuous.

He adjourned to the taproom adjoining a mews at the end of the block and spotted the butler immediately. If you knew your servants, butlers were instantly recognisable, even without their working clothes; the mannerisms of the master without the breeding or, if there was no breeding, without the capital.

There he was, sitting at a copper-topped table, with his arm round a woman in her thirties, probably the housekeeper or the lady's maid. Blackstone guessed that Astor's frugality would be his ally: there would only be a few servants to attend to because he wouldn't employ many.

According to information culled earlier at the taproom, the butler liked both a drink and a gamble. Blackstone sat at a nearby table with a pot of ale, produced a pack of cards and began to play patience.

The butler's eyes swivelled to the cards.

Blackstone was cheating.

The butler frowned, their eyes met and Blackstone, looking embarrassed, said: 'I see I've been caught out.'

The butler, who had polished cheeks and sleek hair greying at the sideburns, favoured him with an expression reserved for tradesmen. 'No sense in cheating yourself.' He returned his attentions to the woman, but Blackstone sensed that he was hooked.

'Would you care for a game?'

The butler frowned and shook his head.

Blackstone sighed and tossed a leather purse on the table. The butler and his lady listened to gold kissing gold.

'Do I play backgammon? Why, it has always been my favourite, ah, sport.'

'Then perhaps we could have a game.'

A backgammon board was produced from behind the bar.

Half an hour later Blackstone had lost the equivalent of twenty dollars. 'One last game,' he said. 'This time for material goods?'

'Material goods?'

'I see you enjoy a drink, sir.'

The butler shrugged. He was dealing with a rich fool, not high in the social order, but high enough to be relieved of more goods and chattels.

One game later the butler had won, in addition to the twenty dollars, two bottles of cognac, one bottle of gin and three bottles of port.

The butler and the woman left the taproom a few minutes later.

After half an hour Blackstone, standing outside 223 Broadway, could hear the sounds of carousing coming from within. Three hours later all was quiet and he judged that the staff were either in a drunken slumber or besporting themselves in each other's bedrooms.

Which left only the night-watchman to attend to.

How do you entice a night-watchman from his post? It wasn't difficult, as Blackstone knew from experience.

It was 1.30 a.m. Time to introduce the harlot he had brought down Broadway from Battery Place. She had already been paid and Blackstone watched from the shadows as she made her approach to the watchman.

He looked startled. As indeed he might, Blackstone reflected, because the girl had been chosen with care – young and black-haired, with breasts bursting from her bodice.

She took the watchman's arm and they vanished down Broadway.

Quietly, Blackstone made his way to the wooden door. It had no visible lock or keyhole, so Blackstone assumed that it was held with bolts on the inside.

From his bag he took the largest house-breaking implement, a brace and bit with a wide-span cutter that could make a hole two feet in diameter. He placed the instrument half way up the door, close to the wall, and began to cut.

A dog came sniffing, a man's footsteps faltered, stopped, continued. Sweat poured down Blackstone's body. He paused and imagined the expression on Birnie's face if he could see him now, or the expressions on the faces of Hays and de Vries, for that matter.

He returned to the task, smelling the sawdust as it fell at his feet. Fear or excitement or both clutched at his bowels and the sweat was cold on his face. He gave the brace and bit a push and the circle of wood gave way, clattering to the floor on the other side of the door. Blackstone froze. A dog barked, a carriage rattled past. Silence.

Blackstone put his arm through the hole and reached upwards. He felt the cold metal of the bolt and pushed it down so that it would slide along, but it was jammed. Blackstone swore. From his bag he took a pot of grease, smeared some on his fingers and ran them along the bolt. He pulled again – and the bolt opened.

Then he reached down and found the bolt holding the bottom of the door. This one moved easily. Blackstone pushed the door and it opened with a creak. Inside, the darkness was impenetrable.

From the bag he took a lantern that he had already lit on a low wick; light only escaped from a hole cut in the metal case. He turned up the wick and a narrow beam of light cut through the darkness.

He stepped inside, closing the door behind him. He was in a short passage that led to another door. Despite the warmth of the night, the air in the passageway was cold and smelt of decay.

To Blackstone it smelt like a miser's hoard. Like the verdigris on coins, like tarnished silver. He could smell money! Blackstone – Captain Kidd – made his way to the second door.

If necessary he would have to repeat the same process on this door, but he didn't want to because he wished to leave the impression that a thief had broken into the passage and had been disturbed before he got any further.

From his bag he selected half a dozen bettys, or picklocks, and an outsider, a pair of pliers with thin jaws which, when inserted into a keyhole, could grasp the end of a key and turn it. Gingerly he inserted a skeleton key. Half an inch into the lock it made contact with the real key, inserted from the other side. Blackstone picked up the pliers and gently felt for the butt end of the key in the lock. The lantern grew hot in his free hand. The jaws of the pliers were round the butt, he twisted them and heard the tumblers turn. The door opened.

A smell of food and alcohol. The beam of light cut the darkness. He was in the hallway and the smell was coming from a flight of stairs leading down to his right – the kitchens and the servants' quarters, he assumed. And that's where the servants would be, he hoped, coaxed into deep sleep by brandy, gin and port.

Now where would John Jacob Astor, a careful and calculating man, keep his secrets?

According to Marryatt – or whoever had broken into the house – the ruby had been in a jewel box in Astor's bedroom. But a man like Astor wouldn't leave jewel cases around when he was away. However, Blackstone wasn't after jewels, not just now. What was he after? A clue, a bright penny that would lead him to a glittering fortune.

In the darkness Blackstone slavered.

He made his way across the hallway to the staircase leading upstairs, the beam from his lantern lighting the eyes of Astors who looked down from oil paintings: brother Henry from whom John Jacob had borrowed five hundred dollars in the early days; his bride, Sarah Todd, from whom he had borrowed three hundred dollars; old man Ashdour at his home in Waldorf.

Blackstone went up the stairs, each creak sounding as loud as a pistol shot. Then he was on a landing. Downstairs he had heard snores, now they seemed louder. Odd.

Gently, he opened a bedroom door. The snores were upon him, two sets of them. And by the light of the moon, flooding in through the window, he saw the butler and the housekeeper asleep in each other's arms. What would John Jacob say?

Blackstone closed the door. While the cat's away...

He opened the door of the next bedroom. A four-poster bed, a dressing-table and a chaise-longue, and beyond them a dressing room and a bathroom. Would a man keep his secrets in the room he shared with his wife? Blackstone doubted it.

Then where?

Ahead lay another small staircase. At the top was a heavy door with a massive lock. Blackstone sighed, put down the lantern and delved into his bag. The lock was a challenge that would have daunted any of the cracksmen who frequented Sol's Tavern.

Blackstone set to work. The first skeleton key he tried was too small. The second one turned without connecting. The third was too big.

Blackstone rested on his haunches. Behind the door lay the secrets. He could feel them, taste them. This is what made you a rich man, John Jacob, he thought. Not furs, not tea, not musical instruments. I am close to your sanctum, John Jacob, to the foundation of your empire. One turn of that lock and I'm as close as one can get to a man's soul.

Panting a little, he tried a fourth skeleton in the massive lock and turned it. For a moment it stuck, then, with a faint grinding sound, it moved and the door was open.

Moonlight lit the attic from a window in the roof. The smell of the place was old and thick, the smell of lives departed, the smell of the tomb. I shouldn't be here, Blackstone thought. I am intruding into the undisturbed past, into the privacy of death, the least a man can expect.

But there was also the smell of money.

Blackstone explored the attic in the bloodless light of the moon. A rack of old clothes that gave off clouds of dust when he touched them, sheaves of parchment, cobwebs hanging from the window.

He found the iron box in a corner, covered with sacking. It was about thirty inches long, sixteen or so inches wide, and encrusted with rust.

On the top, scratched deeply in the metal and just visible through the rust, were two initials.

W.K.

The documents confirmed it – the chest had belonged to Captain Kidd. Blackstone had found them at the bottom of the box and had brought them back to his hotel room.

Now he sat on the edge of his bed, reading them.

Much of the correspondence was from a French-Canadian fur trader named Jacques Cartier, who had apparently worked for Astor at the turn of the century. He had lived part of the year on Deer Isle in Penobscot Bay, where he had experienced 'a remarkable stroke of good fortune'. Duplicates of the letters Astor had sent to Cartier showed how he had ordered the fur trader to return to New York with this 'stroke of good fortune', saying that he would be 'suitably rewarded'.

Blackstone had little doubt that the 'stroke of good fortune' had been the discovery of the iron box containing Kidd's treasure on Deer Isle.

There were also statements from the Manhattan Bank, where Astor had opened an account in 1798. At first the transactions were modest, mostly deposits from the sale of furs. But from 1801 – the time of the correspondence with Carrier – the deposits leapt to massive sums. In one year alone more than five hundred thousand dollars was paid into the account.

Not only that, Blackstone noted, but cheques made out to Jacques Cartier leap-frogged from payments of a few hundred dollars to five thousand dollars.

There were also bank records of cash paid by drafts to Astor, by a Mr Roderick Streeter of London, England. Streeter was apparently a jeweller. In all, he had paid Astor 1,300,000 dollars.

Blackstone drank a glass of water and read on.

Near the bottom of the sheaf of papers was a letter from Streeter acknowledging receipt of diamonds, gold coins, emeralds, pearls – and rubies. Ah, rubies. The lust was upon Blackstone again.

But there was still a host of unanswered questions. Where was the bulk of the treasure now? Did Astor still have it? If the legends about Kidd were true, then Astor had only disposed of a fraction of it to Streeter.

And why were the gems suddenly circulating in London again after an interval of more than twenty years? Perhaps, Blackstone speculated, Astor had decided to get rid of the balance of the treasure because he was getting old and didn't want the true source of his wealth to be discovered after his death.

There was also another minor mystery. Why the hell had Cartier disposed of the legendary fortune for a mere five thousand dollars? The iron box looked as if it had been sawed open. Perhaps Cartier had parted with the box without opening it, and had never appreciated the value of its contents. Perhaps...

Blackstone decided that, if Cartier were still alive, he would have to find him.

He slid the documents beneath the false bottom of one of his travelling cases and lay down on the bed. But he couldn't sleep. Dawn already tinged the skyline with green, and when the light was stronger he re-read a book he had bought about Captain Kidd. According to Sir Cornelius Dalton, Kidd was a 'worthy, honest-hearted, steadfast, much enduring sailor'. According to Lord Bellomont 'there was never a greater liar or thief in the world than this Kidd'.

Blackstone himself took the view that Kidd had been an honest rogue and would have made a fine Bow Street Runner.

According to the book, Kidd had once been a reputable skipper with a fine house in New York, not a pirate like Glover, Tew or Avery. But a merchant named Richard Livingstone had drawn up a plan that was to culminate in Kidd's body swinging in the breeze at Tilbury.

While in London, Livingstone had suggested to five Whig politicians that they back a scheme to put Kidd in command of a ship that would sail the High Seas capturing pirates and, more important, their loot.

One of the principal brains behind the scheme was Lord Bellomont, who had just been made Governor of New York. Everyone was supposed to get a share of the pickings, including, it was rumoured, King William III.

In September 1696 Kidd sailed from New York aboard the *Adventure Galley*. But the pirates were elusive, the crew mutinous, and after a year's abortive patrolling Kidd himself turned pirate.

In January 1697 he captured the Armenian merchantman *Quedah* and took command of it, abandoning the *Adventure Galley* off the coast of Madagascar. In November 1698 an order was made in London that Kidd should be arrested on sight.

From then on every move Kidd made was a disaster. Most of his crew deserted him and when he anchored off Gardiner's Island, New York, on a new vessel, the *San Antonio*, the end was in sight.

According to a statement subsequently made by John Gardiner, the owner of the island, Kidd left behind property including a box of gold, two bags of silver and some gold dust.

Next Kidd went to Boston to meet Bellomont, who double-crossed him. Bellomont – the man who had sent Kidd on the original mission – promised him fair treatment.

After all, Kidd had taken two French ships – he had been authorised to capture pirate ships *and* French vessels – and had the documents to prove it.

Within a few days Bellomont had him clapped in irons. And on 6 April 1700 he was taken ashore at London, to be held in Newgate jail until 8 May 1701.

Kidd had based his defence on the documents taken from the French ships. In effect these proved that he had been carrying out the mission entrusted to him by Bellomont and the other schemers, but although they had been given to Bellomont in America, these documents were never produced at Kidd's trial.

Kidd was charged with the murder of William Moore, his gunner (he killed him by throwing a bucket at him), piracy against the *Quedah* and also piracy against various ships in September, November and December 1697 and January 1698. Nine of his crew were also charged with the general piracy indictments.

The hearing took two days, 8 and 9 May 1701.

And so to Execution Dock on 23 May.

Innocent or guilty?

To Blackstone's way of thinking he was guilty, but guilty of what thousands of other privateers had been engaged in. The tragedy was that his mission had received the blessing of rich, greedy, influential men, and when the plan had gone awry they had absolved their own guilt by sending him to the gibbet.

One final anecdote about Kidd intrigued Blackstone. According to the book, the wretched Mrs Kidd was allowed to see her husband for half an hour after the death sentence had been passed. And, so the story went, he was seen to slip her a card bearing the figures 44106818. The card was later taken from Mrs Kidd, who strenuously denied that she knew the meaning of the figures.

Thoughtfully, Blackstone put down the book and took a map of North America from the travelling bag with the false bottom.

Let us say, Blackstone thought, that the first four figures on the card are a latitude reading and the last four are longitude. He studied the map, frowning and running his hand over the stubble on his chin.

Let us say that the latitude is accurate and that, through some minor inaccuracy in Kidd's chronometer reading, the longitude is fractionally wrong. Let us say it should have read 6813.

If that is so, then Captain Kidd was trying to tell his wife that the treasure was buried on Deer Isle.

CHAPTER NINE

Fanny Campbell was confused.

Crusading for free love and equal rights for women was not as straightforward as she had imagined. She had anticipated male hostility, but she had not anticipated certain nuances of her campaign.

In particular, she had not anticipated any emotional involvement. Nothing wrong with it, of course, except that it weakened her position. However hard she tried, she could not imagine Edmund Blackstone accepting equality in their relationship.

What are my feelings for him, she wondered, as she rode through the countryside on her way from Greenwich to Wall Street. She hoped it was purely physical attraction, for that could be controlled and, when it had spent itself, there would be no regrets.

But if deeper feelings were involved, then there was the danger that she would begin to rely on him, and there was no creature that Fanny Campbell detested more than the swooning, fan-fluttering female, waiting in the drawing-room for an invitation to the ball. That was the tradition from which she had fled. That was why she was in America, the fledgling country where the role of women could be established before it was swamped by male arrogance, as it had been throughout Europe.

She thought about the night she had spent with Blackstone, and immediately spurred her horse at the memory of passion fused with tenderness. It was the tenderness that alarmed her.

The sun was burning the mist from the fields, and cows and horses sought the shade. The leaves on the trees were dull with the prolonged heat. Ahead lay the towers and roof-tops of the city at the tip of the island where white men had first camped. The city was spreading rapidly now, its brick fingers brushing away green farmland. Perhaps one day, mused Fanny, it might even cover the whole island.

She slowed the horse to a trot. Ahead lay a distasteful task. For her campaign – particularly the ballooning – she needed money, and it had begun to look as though she would have to employ 'feminine wiles' to get it.

In Fanny Campbell's book 'feminine wiles' were in the same bracket as attacks of the vapours, an admission that a woman was merely an adornment who had to resort to humiliating subterfuge to get her way.

But, so far, direct approaches for investment in her projects had failed. If she had been a man, of course, it would have been different. Eugene Robertson had been paid twelve hundred dollars for his balloon ascent on 9 July 1825, during the celebrations for the arrival in New York of Lafayette.

She was in the city now, riding past new houses with flat roofs, balconies and stoops. Men were cleaning the streets – they had to be cleaned twice a week by law – and from open windows came the smell of frying ham and coffee.

When she reached Wall Street she tethered the horse. Like any man seeking capital, she had decided to go straight to the top – and John Jacob Astor was very definitely the top. To reach Astor she had to tackle Halleck, and it was with him that she would have to employ 'feminine wiles'.

But Halleck was not alone.

Sitting on one side of his oak desk, which was covered with green leather embossed with gold leaf, there was a big man with a square face, dressed in drab clothes.

Halleck smiled at Fanny and ushered her to an arm-chair. 'I'd like you to meet Mr de Vries,' he said. 'He's a policeman.'

De Vries greeted her clumsily and she sensed that he wasn't at ease with Halleck, the relaxed man-about-town with the practised charm. Fanny sympathised with de Vries. Halleck bored her to distraction.

Halleck said: 'It seems that we've had a little robbery.'

'Robbery? As far as I know, nothing was stolen,' de Vries said, trying to assert himself.

'Oh very well, an attempted robbery then.' Halleck turned to Fanny, who was trying to look demure in the arm-chair. 'Apparently someone tried to break into the home of my lord and master, Mr John Jacob Astor.'

'Oh really?' Fanny was glad that the thief hadn't stolen anything: she didn't want any other drain on Astor's reserves.

Halleck went on: 'Quite a professional job, apparently. The thief used some sort of instrument to cut a hole in a side door, then reached through and undid the bolts from the inside. De Vries', he continued, in patronising tones, 'thinks it was the work of some criminal from England. Apparently they don't have house-breaking implements like that over here.'

'What happened then?' Fanny asked. 'Why didn't they get away with anything?'

De Vries examined his blunt-tipped fingers. 'He seems to have got as far as the inner door. Then he was disturbed. The night-watchman says he heard a noise, but by the time he reached the outside door the thief had run off.'

'He must have been a very ambitious thief', Fanny said, 'to have attempted to break into Mr Astor's house.'

Halleck said to de Vries: 'What was the Watch doing?'

'That's what I want to find out,' de Vries replied, resentment at the question sounding in his voice. 'And I want to know why the night-watchman didn't hear the thief break in.' He stood up. 'Thank you for your help, Mr Halleck.' He bowed to Fanny. 'It's been a pleasure, Miss Campbell.' He paused. 'Thank God nothing was stolen, especially with that Bow Street Runner in town to laugh at us ... '

Halleck looked up. 'Bow Street Runner? What Bow Street Runner?'

De Vries was about to reply when Fanny said: 'You know, the one the gentleman from *The Times* was talking about.'

'Ah,' Halleck said vaguely, 'that Bow Street Runner.'

De Vries left and Halleck turned his attention to Fanny who, after a few pleasantries, came to the point about money. She observed a lizard-like wariness mask Halleck's bland features.

Feminine wiles!

She showed an ankle and suggested to Fitz-Greene Halleck, financial adviser to John Jacob Astor, that if a balloon with a woman as passenger took to the skies with a legend advertising some product emblazoned on its skin, then it could be to Astor's advantage.

Halleck considered this. Finally he told her: 'I don't think it's quite up Mr Astor's street. As you may know, he's primarily concerned with property speculation.'

Fanny did know. It had also occurred to her that Halleck himself might not be averse to an investment. She tossed her ringlets and smiled at him. She wished he would display some of his renowned wit, but she had come to the conclusion that he was one of those who deliver platitudes in a way that passes muster for wit.

'What sort of sum had you in mind?' Halleck asked. 'And what exactly is the point of your ... ah ... campaign?'

Fanny told him about the liberation of the female sex. Halleck looked unhappy about it.

'A thousand dollars would come in handy,' she murmured, showing both ankles.

'A sizeable sum of money.'

She waited.

'I suppose I could toss some money to the winds ...' He smiled. 'Perhaps we could, ah, have lunch together and discuss terms ...'

And so to bed, Fanny thought. But another plan was materialising in her mind. It concerned Edmund Blackstone. Why had he been 'interviewing' Halleck?

Imagining Halleck trying to be witty in bed, she made a sudden decision. She would put her proposition to Blackstone. She stood up. 'Thank you for your consideration, Mr Halleck, but I've decided not to throw discretion to the winds.'

'But—'

'I have another appointment.'

She allowed him to kiss her hand, then left his chambers in search of the self-appointed representative of *The Times*.

But Blackstone was missing.

In fact he was engaged upon a manhunt. For a man who might well be dead. Jacques Cartier, the man to whom Astor had paid five thousand dollars.

Blackstone went first to City Hall, but there was no record of any Jacques Cartier living in New York. Even if he were alive, he could be anywhere in America, in the world for that matter. He was a French Canadian, so there was a strong likelihood that he had returned to Quebec. But there was just a chance ...

Blackstone headed for the quayside tavern where the French-Canadian whore had tried to rob him. She greeted him without enthusiasm. Blackstone rekindled her interest by giving her a dollar and buying her a drink. He also kept a tight hold on his purse.

They sat outside, at a wooden table on the cobblestones. It was midday and the quayside was thronged with seamen, merchants, chandlers, agents, watermen – and thieves. On the ships moored at the quay cargoes were being loaded and unloaded, carpenters banged away with hammers, painters sloshed paint around and seamen swarmed the rigging. Beyond, on the still waters of the bay, great sailing ships were becalmed, while steamboats hurried between them.

Blackstone said: 'I want your help.'

'Something to cure the pox?' She giggled and her gypsy ear-rings bobbed.

'I want to know where French Canadians congregate in this city.'

'Sometimes they come here,' she said in her twangy voice, 'to see me.'

'Ever hear of a man called Jacques Cartier?'

She frowned. 'I don't think so. Why do you want to know? Are you some sort of policeman?' she asked, leaning across the table.

'Do I look like one?'

'In a way. And in a way you don't – in fact, in a way you look a bit of a villain.'

An astute girl, Blackstone decided. 'Where else do French Canadians go?'

'If I tell you, you'll leave me.'

Blackstone gave her another dollar, bought her another drink and told her: 'I'll come back.'

'Perhaps we could have some fun together. This time I won't try and steal your money. Unless, of course, you want to give me a little something ... '

'We'll see.' Blackstone grinned at her. 'Now, where do the French Canadians go?' He had an inspiration. 'Where would I find fur traders from Quebec?'

'That's easy,' she said, and directed him to a tavern near Washington Square, the site where criminals were hanged and buried. 'But hurry back.'

'I will.'

The bar was a spartan place, with a few tables and chairs on a sawdust-covered floor; strictly for drinking, with no concessions to social niceties. A few men in shirt-sleeves and fur boots sat at the tables, drinking. They had seamed faces and most of them were bearded.

Blackstone ordered a pot of ale from a waiter and asked him if he knew Jacques Cartier.

The waiter, who had a barrel chest and arms strongly muscled from throwing customers into the street, said: 'Who wants to know?'

'I do.'

'And who might you be?' The waiter put down his tray and folded his arms, making his biceps bulge. 'That's a pretty fancy accent you've got, mister. Not the sort of accent we're used to in here.'

'It's an English accent,' Blackstone said, 'the reason being that I'm English.'

'Pretty fancy, huh?'

'Pretty,' Blackstone agreed.

'Then I suggest you drink your ale and find some pretty bar where they like pretty voices.'

Blackstone sighed. A fist-fight wouldn't inspire revelations about Cartier's whereabouts. He gave the waiter a dollar.

'Pretty and mean, huh?'

Blackstone gave him another dollar.

'Is that for the ale?'

'That's for you – and another two if you tell me where I can find Jacques Cartier.'

'I asked who wants him?'

'My name's Whitestone.'

'Pretty fancy name,' the waiter said.

'Do you know him?'

'I might. Why do you want him?'

'I have some information which might be to his advantage.'

'He could sure use something to his advantage,' the waiter conceded.

'Is he in trouble?' 'He might be.'

'What sort of trouble?'

'Five dollars' worth,' the waiter said, ignoring demands for service from other customers.

'That's pretty expensive trouble.'

'You want to know pretty bad, mister. That's the price.'

'Tell me one thing – is he in New York?'

'He might be.' The waiter spat on the sawdust. 'And then again, he might not be.'

'Your information better be good.'

'Don't threaten me,' the waiter said. 'In this place no one threatens me.'

'If I give you three more dollars you'll tell me? No more upping the price?'

'You give me the three dollars and you'll find out, mister.'

Blackstone handed him three more dollars. 'Now, where's Jacques Cartier?'

'Up near the canal.'

'The Erie Canal?'

'That's the only canal I know of, mister.' 'Whereabouts on the canal?' 'You can't do much with five dollars these days.'

'Whereabouts?'

The waiter pocketed the money. 'Take a walk along the canal, mister. You can't miss him.'

Blackstone stood up. 'The canal', he said quietly, 'is three hundred and sixty miles long.'

'That's right – the longest in the world.'

'Whereabouts on the canal?'

'Another two dollars could shake my memory.'

'All right.' Blackstone slipped his right hand into the left-hand inside pocket of his jacket. He hit the waiter on the jaw with his right elbow, then his right fist, following through with his left fist and left elbow.

The waiter stared at him from the floor for a moment before going for his knife. Blackstone kicked it across the floor. Then he put his foot on the waiter's throat. 'Whereabouts on the canal?' he asked.

The waiter choked.

'Whereabouts?' Blackstone released the pressure on his throat. The waiter grabbed at his foot and Blackstone kicked him in the kidneys. The waiter grunted. 'Where?'

'Albany. In a shack – you can't miss it.' The waiter described the shack.

'Thank you.' Blackstone bent down and removed the five dollars from the waiter's pocket. He slapped the money on the table and said to the other customers: 'Drinks on the house.'

The waiter struggled to his hands and knees, swearing.

'That isn't pretty, mister,' Blackstone said, pushing him with one foot and sending him sprawling.

He hurried out of the tavern.

Jacques Cartier was about sixty, with most of the symptoms of chronic drunkenness: halting speech, as though listening to what he was saying, trembling hands, deep lines in the undernourished flesh of his face, vague eyes. There was stubble on his chin and his grey hair was unevenly cropped. He spoke a little English, with a thick accent.

His home was indeed a shack, crudely built from timber, furnished with an unmade bed, a table, two chairs, a wooden chest and an iron stove, the ash of winter still cold in its mouth.

Cartier was sitting outside in the afternoon sunshine, gazing towards the canal, a few hundred yards away, which linked Lake Erie with New York via the Hudson.

The canal interested Blackstone. It was progress, part of the process that might one day lift the under-privileged from the slums – if the privileged didn't pinch all the loot first. Blackstone would like to have met Governor DeWitt Clinton, who had proposed the idea in 1809 and who, sixteen years later, had ceremonially emptied a bucket of water from the lake into the Atlantic.

Cartier didn't have the hallmarks of a man interested in progress. He looked as if he were waiting to die. He was dressed in moulting fur boots, torn trousers and a dirty blue shirt.

Blackstone wasn't sure how to handle him.

He sat down on a boulder facing Cartier, who was hunched in a rocking-chair, and introduced himself. Cartier didn't respond.

Blackstone said: 'I believe you used to live on Deer Isle?' There was a slight shift of expression on the loose features. 'What you want?'

Blackstone decided to storm straight in. 'I believe you once worked for John Jacob Astor.'

'So?' Cartier began to tremble – fear, fever or booze? Blackstone wasn't sure. He handed the old fur trader his silver hip-flask of brandy. Cartier guzzled greedily and the trembling subsided.

'I believe you once sold Astor an iron box.'

Cartier looked crafty. 'I may have done. What of it?'

'I think you should have been paid more for it. I can get you more. And here's some to start with,' said Blackstone, handing Cartier fifty dollars, enough to keep him in liquor till Christmas. 'In return,' Blackstone said, 'I want you to tell me all you can about the transaction with Astor. For instance, did you know what was in that box?'

Cartier thought about it, reached a decision. He drank some more brandy, reviving with its illusory strength. He nodded. 'Treasure.'

'Did you know how much treasure?'

'It must 'ave been much. He pay me five thousand dollars.'

'And you think that was a lot of money?'

'Five thousand dollars. That's a lot of money, no?'

'It depends,' Blackstone said. 'It depends on how much you think was in that box.'

Cartier shrugged. 'Maybe three times that much?'

Blackstone said: 'Maybe a thousand times that much. Maybe more,' he added, watching the expression change on Cartier's face. Then he asked: 'Do you think you received fair payment?'

Patches of red appeared on Cartier's cheeks. 'You think I was cheated?'

'Not cheated. Astor is a businessman. He offered you a sum of money and you accepted. A fair business deal, I should say. Except, of course, that you should have received a hundred thousand dollars. As a result, Astor is a millionaire and you...' Blackstone gestured at the wooden shack. 'You are not quite so well off.'

Cartier slumped further in the rocking-chair. He said: 'It's too late now. What can I do?' He took a long pull at the hip-flask.

'I told you what you can do. You can tell me everything you know about the box. You can show me any letters you had from Astor.'

'Letters?'

'You wrote to each other, didn't you?'

Cartier shook his head. 'I can't read or write...'

'But Astor has letters from you...'

A shadow of cunning touched Cartier's face and he asked: 'How you know?'

'It doesn't matter,' Blackstone said, 'but I do know.'

'I didn't write them. I had them written for me.'

'And you got replies?'

Cartier nodded. 'I got replies. Two I think.'

'Are they here?'

'Somewhere I think.'

'Then perhaps...'

'In a minute,' said Cartier, tilting the flask. 'We have time. Not many people talk to me these days.'

Blackstone said: 'Tell me about the box, how you found it...'

In between swigs from the flask, Cartier described in halting English how he had discovered Captain Kidd's treasure.

At the turn of the century Cartier had been fur trading with the Indians on the shores of the Penobscot River and he stored the pelts on the southern tip of Deer Isle, before travelling to New York to sell them. On the island he had come across a cave in the rocks, about ten feet high and reaching back twenty-five feet. At high tide it was submerged, but at low tide you could walk into it.

One morning Cartier entered the cave and noticed that a strong tide had shifted the sand. Protruding from the blue clay underneath was the top of the iron box. He manhandled the box out of the cave and took it with his furs to New York, where he sold it to Astor.

Later he bought a few acres of land on Deer Isle and lived there in a log hut with his Indian wife. But, because he no longer worked, spending his time hunting and fishing – and drinking – the island inhabitants suspected that he was a thief. Life on the island became difficult and he came south, first to Boston and finally, striking west, to Albany.

Blackstone told Cartier that he didn't understand why he had parted with the box without opening it.

Cartier peered into the empty flask as though it were a telescope, shook it in disbelief and handed it back to Blackstone.

He said: 'It was a gamble.'

'Did you know Kidd's treasure was inside it?'

'I was not sure. But it would have taken long time to open it and I 'ad to get to New York on time. Astor did not like men to be late ... '

'Couldn't you have opened it in New York?'

'Perhaps. But suppose it had been empty? Suppose it was fill with rocks. Then there was no gamble. And Astor – he would have seen that the box had been open because you had to open it with a ... ' Cartier did a mime with one hand.

'A saw?'

'Yes,' Cartier said, 'a saw, that's it.'

'And that's all you got, five thousand dollars?'

'There were a few other payments,' Cartier conceded.

'And the letters...'

'Letters?' Cartier stared at Blackstone with his rheumy eyes. 'What letters?'

'You said you had some from Astor.'

'*Oui*, I 'ave them.'

Cartier stood up and made his way unsteadily into the shack. Blackstone stayed in the fresh air.

Ten minutes later Cartier returned with two yellowing documents, stained and nibbled by mice. He handed them to Blackstone. They were the originals of the letters he had founded duplicated among Astor's papers.

Blackstone handed them back to Cartier. Now what? He had travelled all the way to Albany on the treasure trail, and Cartier had confirmed the theory about Astor's riches. But, he reflected, I'm no nearer to dipping my hands into a pile of lustrous pearls, sparkling diamonds, gleaming gold... And yet I'm sure that Astor must have a hoard hidden somewhere, because he has started dispatching jewels to London again.

'Is that everything?' Blackstone asked Cartier. 'No more letters, nothing more to tell me?'

Cartier told him that there was nothing more.

Blackstone stood up and stretched. 'Thanks for your help. I'll get the stage back to New York,' he said, and was about to stride away when he realised that Cartier was hesitating.

Cartier said: 'Is it true?'

'Is what true?'

'Is it true that you can find more treasure?'

'I think it might be,' Blackstone said. 'I thought—'

'Then take this.' From inside his shirt Cartier took a sheet of cracked parchment that had been pieced together and stuck on a roll of canvas. 'You see, there was another box – a very small box. I keep that box.' Cartier came closer to Blackstone, breathing brandy fumes into his face. 'In that box I find this. You have it. For me it is too late ... '

He gave Blackstone the roll of canvas. On the parchment was a map of an island.

A house across the street from the Eagle Hotel was on fire and when Blackstone got back Fanny Campbell was standing at the hotel entrance watching the firemen at work.

She greeted Blackstone and said: 'I want to have a chat with you.'

'What about?'

'Balloons, 'she said.

'It was probably a child's paper balloon that set that house on fire. They catch fire at a certain height, apparently.'

'It isn't paper balloons I want to discuss.'

'Ah,' he said.

There were three engines and hose-carriers outside the blazing house. The hoses were sucking water from the bay and the jets arched high into the flames. Two helmeted firemen wearing red shirts and dark trousers were carrying an old man out of the front door.

'Isn't it about time they had female firemen?' Blackstone asked.

'Why not? And female Bow Street Runners perhaps.'

The foreman of the firemen was shouting orders, through a trumpet, to douse the adjoining house with water, to stop the flames spreading. The fire looked as if it was under control.

'Let's go and have a drink,' Blackstone said.

'You drink too much.'

'I know it,' he said.

They had a drink in the hotel lounge, then adjourned to Blackstone's room, where they led each other to the bed with scrupulous equality.

Afterwards, lying in bed, watching sparks from the dying blaze drift past the window, Fanny put her proposition to him. Could he help finance a balloon expedition?

Blackstone took it philosophically. Usually it was the man who took advantage of the woman in pursuit of worldly goods. But not with Fanny Campbell.

He asked her: 'What makes you think I've got any money?'

'You have a certain reputation in England. One assumes that you are well paid. After all, it's rumoured that men like Townsend have made fortunes. And you are one of the most famous of the Runners at the moment, aren't you, Blackie?' She snuggled close to him.

'Aye, that's as may be. But what blunt I've got is in England.'

'Why did you come to America?' she asked, propping herself up on one elbow and staring into his eyes.

'You know why I came here – to advise the New York High Constable on how to conduct his business.'

'Mmmmmmm... Then why were you posing as a correspondent of *The Times* with Halleck?'

'Because I don't want every Tom, Dick and Harry to know my business.'

'But what harm can that do? You're here on official business, Blackie.' She paused, breasts brushing Blackstone's chest, then said: 'I wonder—'

'Just what the hell do you wonder?'

'I wonder whether your ... your approach to Halleck had anything to do with the fact that he's financial adviser to John Jacob Astor?'

'And why should you think that?' Blackstone swung himself out of bed, because there is no equality when you're lying on your back being interrogated by a girl who is stroking your chest with her breasts.

'Because it also occurred to me.'

'What occurred to you?' Blackstone asked, putting on a scarlet silk dressing-gown and sitting down in a chair.

'It occurred to me to go to Halleck and ask him for money for my project.'

'And did he rise?'

'He might. But I thought I'd find out your reactions first.'

'Simple. Take Halleck's money.'

She sat up in bed, hands feeling her breasts. Blackstone wished she would stop. She pulled the blanket up to her neck, asking: 'Did you know there had been a burglary at Astor's house?'

'No,' Blackstone said, reaching for his snuff-box, 'I didn't.'

'But nothing was stolen.'

'Really?'

'So I wonder why the thief broke in?'

'Perhaps he was disturbed.'

'Perhaps. But it seems odd that the watchman didn't catch him breaking in. Why didn't he disturb him when he was inside the house?'

Blackstone took some snuff and shrugged. 'Who knows ... Perhaps he was asleep when the break-in was made.'

'And another thing,' Fanny said, 'the break-in was done by an expert.'

'You seem to know a lot about it,' Blackstone observed.

'De Vries told me.'

'Oliver Cromwell,' Blackstone said.

'I beg your pardon?'

'He reminds me of Oliver Cromwell, without the warts. What else did he say?'

'He said the thief was disturbed in a passage leading to the main hall of the house.'

'Unlucky,' Blackstone said.

'He also said he thought the burglar came from England.'

'Really? And why should he think that?'

'Because the instruments he used are favoured by English criminals.'

'Ah.'

'I expect you 'd be able to confirm that, Blackie.'

'I expect so,' Blackstone said.

More sparks floated past the window as Fanny Campbell remarked: 'I suppose it's just a coincidence ... '

'What's a coincidence?'

'That you were pretending to be a correspondent of *The Times* with Halleck, who is financial adviser to Astor, whose house was broken into by an expert thief, who used a house-breaking tool favoured by English thieves.'

'A remarkable coincidence,' Blackstone agreed.

'I'm having dinner with Mr Hays,' she said.

'*Bon appétit*,' Blackstone said.

'Can you help me with my project?'

'I'll think about it,' he said.

And later he did, thinking that it would be a good idea to launch Fanny Campbell in her balloon one day when a wind was gusting strongly out to sea.

Chapter Ten

Blackstone spent the next couple of days advising Hays about the methods of the Bow Street Runners in London and diverting inquiries about Sir Robert Peel and his plans for a uniformed police force.

He liked the tough High Constable who extracted confessions with corpses and they exchanged theories on criminal detection: the value of informers; the use of two interrogators – one hostile and one friendly, to confuse the prisoner; the possibilities of matching bullets with the gun from which they were fired; the ploy of promising to ease up on a suspect if he peached on his colleagues...

Hays feared the worst for New York and blamed the authorities for not vetting immigrants adequately. 'We need the new blood to build our town,' he was fond of observing, 'but we don't need the bad blood.'

He was dubious about the guns that Blackstone carried. 'If we use guns then the criminals will use them.'

And Blackstone replied: 'If I didn't carry a barker, then every thief in London would dance at my funeral.'

'I've survived,' Hays told him, grasping his staff.

'Aye,' Blackstone said, 'but this is a village compared with London. Everyone knows you. If I waved a staff at some villain from Shadwell who'd never set eyes on me before, he'd put a ball straight through my heart.'

'But what about your baton? I've heard it puts the fear of God into every criminal in England.'

'True,' Blackstone agreed. 'But it doesn't have much power over a gang of armed footpads you've just cornered.'

In the evenings – except on the one when Hays gave a dinner party for Fanny Campbell – the two men adjourned to the tavern near the Bowery Theatre.

There was considerable excitement in the tavern one evening over events at the theatre. There had been several protests about the 'new-style French dancing' by Madame Francisque Hutin from Paris, and de Vries had asked Hays to close the place down. According to one newspaper, members of the audience had departed 'crimson with shame' when Madame Hutin had shown a leg.

Hays, who had been present, had not left.

Subsequently he *was* almost crimson with shame. Because Madame Hutin had turned out to be a man!

'And I admired her damned ankles,' Hays confided to Blackstone in the tavern. 'What do you make of that?'

Blackstone told him and, after a pause, Hays laughed. 'It was a neat ankle though – for a man.' He drank some ale. 'At least there's no mistaking the sex of your friend Miss Campbell.'

Blackstone agreed warily.

'She seems to be a great admirer of yours.'

'She does?'

'She talked about you quite a bit the other night.'

Blackstone regarded Hays over the brim of his tankard. 'Really? What did she say?'

'She said I should put you in charge of the inquiries into the break-in at Astor's house. You know, because de Vries thinks the job was pulled by an English villain and you would know how to handle it.' He paused. 'Fancy the job?'

'I'll look into it,' Blackstone assured him.

'It was a funny kind of job. Very professional, and yet amateurish. You know, what sort of guy makes such a racket in a passage that the watchman hears him?'

'A bungling burglar,' Blackstone said. 'But he shouldn't be hard to find in Manhattan – if he's still here. Put some pressure on your local villains – they'll tell us what English thieves are operating over here.'

'I'll hand them over to you,' Hays said. 'It's your case from now on.'

They spent three such nights in the tavern and it was after the third that Blackstone was attacked.

He was walking down Wall Street, a copy of the *Evening Post* under his arm, and had just reached a corner opposite the Custom House where a certain C. Pool ran a business in law books. The gas lamps were pouring out their white light, but one had been knocked out, possibly with a stone thrown by a street urchin.

As Blackstone moved from the light to the darkness he sensed the blow coming from behind and moved his head quickly, so that the truncheon struck his shoulder. He flung himself to one side, reaching for the pistol in his belt with his right hand. But there were two of them, maybe three.

One grasped his shooting arm. He saw the truncheon raised again. He managed to ram his knee into the groin of the man holding his arm and ducked under the blow from the truncheon, butting the assailant in the belly.

Then it was a free-for-all, with the odds against Blackstone. As fists and truncheon smashed into his face and boots thudded into his legs, he decided that his only hope was to fire the pistol to bring help.

The pistol had fallen from the darkness into the gaslight. Blackstone caught a flailing leg with one hand

and jerked upwards, sending the man crashing on to his back.

Then he was diving for the gun, vomit sour in his mouth, pain expanding inside him.

A boot thudded into his ribs. Why the hell hadn't he brought the pocket pistol? Another boot knocked him sideways and he was aware that one of the attackers was grabbing for the pistol.

He remembered the hotel thief whose skull had been cracked open off the Ratcliffe Highway; he remembered Captain Kidd and thought he might be joining him; he was surprised he wasn't going to die on the end of a rope...

These thoughts occupied a fraction of a second.

They were cut short by an explosion and a flash of light that seemed to illuminate the interior of his skull. So this was death.

And yet there were the stars.

And the sound of running feet. And shouts. And a groan from nearby.

Blackstone managed to turn his head. In the gaslight lay a man's body, pistol in hand, blood pumping rhythmically from a hole in his chest.

Blackstone's last conscious thought was that he was glad that the dying man hadn't realised the pistol had a hairspring trigger and that, if handled clumsily when cocked, it would fire.

He came to in the premises of C. Pool, Law Books.

There were several faces above him and the first one he recognised was de Vries.

De Vries said: 'You were lucky. The Watch was nearby and they heard the shot.'

Blackstone examined himself and de Vries told him: 'No bones broken – the doc's had a look at you,' nodding at a pink-faced, white-haired man delving into a black bag.

Blackstone looked at the other men clustered around, presumably members of the Watch and as villainous-looking as any of the customers at Bow Street.

De Vries asked: 'Have you any idea why you were attacked?'

Blackstone shook his head painfully. 'Perhaps the criminals don't approve of Bow Street Runners advising the High Constable on how to catch them.' He could smell burning tallow from a candle on a table and ink from the piles of books around him. 'Did you catch any of them?'

'Only him.' De Vries pointed at a body on the floor. 'A notorious footpad. The motive may have been robbery.'

Blackstone described the captain of the frigate, asking: 'Did you see anyone answering that description?'

De Vries shook his head. 'But Hays tells me you've taken over the investigation into the Astor break-in. That might be the reason for the assault. Maybe they thought you were on to something.'

One of Blackstone's eyes had closed, his ribs ached and he could taste blood. 'Maybe,' he said.

'Well,' de Vries said, labouring at a joke, 'it's beginning to look as if we should come to London to advise Bow Street.'

'Isn't it,' Blackstone said. De Vries, he thought, looked like a cross between a preacher and a fist-fighter.

'Now we'll get you back to your hotel and the doctor can get to work on you there. I've got my carriage outside,' he added.

They helped Blackstone to his feet and he walked into the night air, which was still hot after the day's fever. He heard the cry of a vendor selling clams. He felt pain. He knew that, even if he failed to find the treasure, he had to find the men who had given him the pain.

That was the first attempt on Blackstone's life. The second was set in motion two days later and it was nicely calculated, Blackstone being stiff from the beating, one eye still partially closed.

The man chosen for the attempt was named Laxton and his profession was killing.

Laxton was a professional duellist from the South. He could fight moderately well with swords, but he preferred guns and, because survival was the essence of his profession, he discreetly withdrew from contests where the blade instead of the ball had been chosen.

He was a quiet man with sallow features and a rare smile, that was transformed into a snarl by a scar from a sabre wound in the early days, when he had ill-advisedly chosen the blade.

Laxton was not merely a skilled practitioner of his craft, he was also a student of it. When he wasn't duelling or travelling to a duel or cleaning his pistols, he was reading accounts of duels. One of his favourites was the marathon between DeWitt Clinton and Swarthout in New York in 1802. He wasn't impressed by the skill of the two men, but he was fascinated by their relentless courage.

Three times shots were exchanged. Swarthout was asked: 'Are you satisfied, sir?' and he replied: 'I am not, neither shall I be until the apology is made which I have demanded. Until then we must proceed.' Clinton was asked to sign an apology but refused to do so, adding that he would shake hands with Swarthout because they were friends. Swarthout declined.

So to the fourth shot. Swarthout was hit five inches below the left knee-cap. While a surgeon extracted the ball from Swarthout's leg there was another verbal exchange – with the same result.

The fifth shot. This time Swarthout was hit in the same leg, five inches above the ankle. Again he refused to quit unless he received an apology. But Clinton, not being of a murderous disposition, refused to continue.

Whenever he read the account of the duel, Laxton was puzzled by Clinton's withdrawal when faced with a sitting duck. In Laxton's dreams he took careful aim at the crippled Swarthout and shot him through the heart.

Laxton also knew every detail of the famous duel at Weehawken, New Jersey, on 11 July 1804, between Alexander Hamilton, George Washington's friend, and Aaron Burr, Vice-President of the United States and leader of the Democrats. Hamilton was said to have described Burr as 'a dangerous man, and one who ought not to be trusted with the reigns of government'. He refused to apologise, on the grounds that the statement 'came fairly within the bounds prescribed in cases of political animosity'.

After the signal was given at Weehawken, on the ledge above the Hudson, Hamilton pitched forward mortally wounded. As a result Burr became an outcast and died destitute on Staten Island in September 1836.

Again Laxton was puzzled – by Hamilton's attitude. Before the duel he had written a paper regretting the duel, because of religious and moral principles, because his wife, children and creditors would suffer if he died, because he bore Burr no ill will outside politics, and because 'I shall hazard much, and can possibly gain nothing'. As he was dying he also forgave Burr, which was beyond the comprehension of Burr who forgave no one.

Laxton was intrigued, like everyone else, by the duel between Charles Dickinson and General Andrew Jackson.

Intrigued because, like himself, they were both crack shots.

Jackson had accused Dickinson of slandering his wife. At the outset of the duel, Dickinson raised his pistol and fired, and dust flew from the front of Jackson's coat. But Jackson didn't fall and Dickinson shouted: 'Great God, have I missed him?' Jackson then fired, killing Dickinson, and only at that point was it noticed that one of Jackson's shoes was filled with blood.

It was discovered that Dickinson's ball had hit him in the chest, breaking two ribs. In later years admiration of Jackson's courage was touched with cynicism, when it was suggested that he had dressed in a loose-fitting coat to mislead Dickinson: had he worn his usual clothes the bullet would have penetrated his heart.

Again there were issues beyond Laxton's comprehension. Jackson – Old Hickory – had issued his challenge because of his deep love for his wife. Laxton loved no one. But he did love money and killing, and that was why he had travelled to New York from Buffalo, where he had been employed to kill a cuckolded husband.

The pay for the New York assignment was good and the instructions were routine: provoke the victim, manipulate the exchange so that he issues a challenge, kill him at dawn.

The victim on this occasion was to be an Englishman named Edmund Blackstone.

Sitting in his room in a lodging house in the small settlement of Harlem, Laxton planned his strategy while he cleaned and oiled his guns. Blackstone was an unknown quantity, because he was English and Laxton had never killed an Englishman. But he had been told that Blackstone was a ladies' man and was courting a girl named Fanny Campbell.

Perhaps he could force Blackstone to issue a challenge by insulting the girl. This had advantages and disadvantages. The advantage, as always, was that Laxton, the challenged party, could choose his weapons; the disadvantage was that Blackstone, if he didn't recognise the code of gentlemen, might reply by knocking him to the ground.

Certainly Laxton had to be called, because it wasn't merely his prowess with pistols that made him prefer them to swords: it was the care with which his own guns had been doctored. According to the duelling code, rifling of the barrel of a pistol was forbidden. Laxton flouted this rule by using pistols that were rifled at the breech but not at the muzzle. His pistols were also fitted with every refinement favoured by the professional duellist – hydraulic barrel-tester, recessed breech for rapid fire and hair-spring trigger.

The other sophistication of Laxton's performance on the duelling field was his ability to flout as many of the twenty-six laws of the *code duello*, drawn up in Ireland in 1777, as possible. And in case any objection was made to his behaviour, he would have a fast horse waiting nearby.

He finished oiling a brace of pistols and replaced them gently in the cushioned compartments of their case.

Then he stood up and gazed out of the window in the direction of Manhattan Toe. There was a lot to be done within the next few days – inspect Weehawken duelling ground, assess the abilities of his opponent and extract the first payment from his employer.

At the thought of the money Laxton smiled. He glanced in the tin mirror on the wall and a sallow-faced man in black snarled back.

CHAPTER ELEVEN

I t should have occurred to him before.

Blackstone, sitting on a bench on the Battery reading *The Spy* by James Fenimore Cooper, put the book down and gazed across the bay.

If he was officially in charge of the investigation into the burglary at Astor's house, then he was in a privileged position to pursue his treasure hunt. He could return to the house, he could even interview John Jacob.

But he would have to make sure that Halleck wasn't present to identify him as a correspondent of *The Times*. Blackstone suspected that he had unnecessarily complicated his position.

I'm not operating at my best, Blackstone decided. First the sea-sickness, then the beating in Wall Street. And all the time the heat. A breath of wind, he thought, would be as effective as smelling salts.

He stood up and strolled towards Castle Garden. He smiled at two pretty girls and was perturbed by their reaction – until he remembered his half-closed eye, split lip and grazed cheek.

He touched the bruised eye. Why had he been attacked? A routine robbery by a gang of footpads? A conspiracy to have him killed by the captain of the frigate? Or a conspiracy by someone who knew that he was on the trail of Captain Kidd's loot...

Blackstone sauntered into Castle Garden, where placards advertised a shooting match. The prize was two wolves, 'highly domesticated'.

He sat down at a table in the lounge and ordered a pot of ale. In the background the violinists tried to saw through the heat. From his pocket he took the map that Cartier had given him. An island. What island? Where? It had no scale and therefore could be five hundred miles long or just a rock in an archipelago.

He put the map away and stood up as Fanny Campbell arrived, as cool as an iceberg in a tropic sea. She expressed concern at his injuries. He ordered her a glass of mint tea and slid an envelope across the table. Inside the envelope was two hundred and fifty dollars. The situation, he thought, had deteriorated badly when he had to buy a girl's silence.

She picked up the envelope. 'How much?'

He told her. 'That's all I can afford.'

'At the moment?'

'What do you mean by that?'

'I imagine you have some expectations...'

'You might at least say thank you.'

'Thank you,' she said, touching his arm and smiling. 'That will help finance the first meeting.'

'What first meeting?'

'I'm starting a series of lectures on equality. You know—'

'Yes,' Blackstone interrupted, 'I know.'

She handed him a copy of a newspaper. 'It seems that my ideas don't have everyone's approval.'

Blackstone read that Miss Fanny Campbell was 'a bold blasphemer and a voluptuous preacher of licentiousness'.

'An observant reporter,' Blackstone commented.

'Perhaps you'd like to dispatch your comments to *The Times*...'

'They wouldn't print them,' Blackstone said.

She sipped her tea and asked: 'Just what *are* you up to in New York, Blackie?'

'You know perfectly well.'

'Trying to rob Astor?'

'That's slanderous.' Blackstone said. 'As a matter of fact I'm in charge of the case. I think Hays wants to find out just how good the Bow Street Runners are.'

'Supposing you catch the thief – won't that put you in an awkward position?'

'Why should it?' Blackstone asked.

'Mightn't you run the risk of arresting yourself?'

'A wrongful arrest,' Blackstone said. 'I would take legal action against myself.'

'And who would win?'

'Edmund Blackstone, of course.' Blackstone, who wasn't enjoying the joke, changed the topic of conversation. 'You're going to need police protection at that meeting of yours. Every Puritan in town will be against you.'

'Every arrogant male, you mean.'

The violinists swung into patriotic songs of the War of Independence and Blackstone told her: 'Not necessarily. Mrs Smith, content with her husband who returns dutifully every evening, will be against you too, because she won't want the security of her home jeopardised by free love beckoning to her old man as he plods home from his carpenter's bench.'

'It beckons from every tavern and sidewalk as it is.'

'Ah.' Blackstone wagged his finger at her. 'But Mr Smith is not the sort of fellow to go with loose women. What's more, he can't afford to. But if some little playmate – his workmate's sister or daughter, one of your disciples, per-haps – beckons, then that would be a very different kettle of fish.'

'Every revolutionary movement has met opposition,' said the viking woman beside him, with a toss of her flaxen ringlets. And then, more thoughtfully: 'Do you go with loose women, Blackie?'

'Of course,' he said, promptly.

'Ah.' She was silent.

'You should be pleased.'

'Why should I be pleased?'

'Because you're advocating all women being loose.' He held up a hand to silence her. 'It depends on your definition of *loose*. When you say loose you mean women who sleep with men frequently. You use the word in a derogatory sense and yet you 're campaigning for it.'

'When I refer to loose women,' Fanny Campbell said, 'I mean women who accept money while allowing men to use their bodies.'

'What about the bawds, strumpets and harlots who visit the taverns and sleep with men because they *like* it?'

'The conversation', she said, 'is becoming distasteful. I meant women who take money.'

'In that case,' Blackstone said self-righteously, 'I haven't been with loose women.'

'How very uninteresting,' she said.

'Have you told Hays about the meeting?'

'He already knows. He said there might be trouble – but he was much more understanding than you.'

'He likes a pretty ankle, does Hays. Even if it turns out to be a male ankle.'

'I beg your pardon?'

'It doesn't matter,' Blackstone said. 'When is the meeting?'

'In four days time. You don't have to attend.'

'I wouldn't dream of missing it. I've always been partial to a riot.'

'Not in the state you 're in, I shouldn't think. Have you any idea why you were attacked?'

Blackstone said he had no idea. In all probability it was a gang of common thieves.

'You haven't been very convincing with your advice to the High Constable.'

Blackstone shrugged; it was true. He paid the waiter and told Fanny that he had important business to attend to – which was true, because Halleck was approaching and it seemed the ideal time to interview John Jacob Astor.

Fanny nodded perfunctorily as Halleck sat down, her attention distracted by another man who had hastily paid his bill when Blackstone rose to leave and was following him out of the lounge. He was dressed in black but, unlike de Vries, he didn't invite comparison with the clergy. In fact he looked more like an undertaker seeking custom. His features were sallow and there was a curious twist to his mouth. Fanny Campbell resolved to tell Blackstone about him; then she turned her attention to Halleck.

The butcher's son from Waldorf, near Heidelberg in the Grand Duchy of Baden, was sitting at his desk in his study, drinking a tumbler of mineral water.

He was in his sixties, grey-haired, well-built, healthy, wary. There was an aura of power about him, but Blackstone wasn't sure whether this stemmed from his physical presence or the knowledge that he was one of the richest men in the world. If you're told someone is a power in the land, then you tend to be impressed by his personality before you've tested it.

Even before Blackstone had sat down opposite him, Astor had indicated, without speaking, that he could only spare a few minutes. A hurried scrawl of a signature on a legal document, impatient movements of papers on his desk, a glance at his pocket watch.

Finally he said: 'I have a business appointment in ten minutes. Can you please come to the point. In fact I don't quite see the necessity for this meeting...' He spoke English with a thick German accent.

Blackstone began to explain that he was investigating the attempted burglary but was interrupted – 'Quite, I know all about that. Hays told me. For the life of me I can't see why he or de Vries can't deal with it.'

'Because', Blackstone said, controlling himself, 'they believe an English criminal tried to break into your house and I am something of an expert in that direction.'

Astor grunted. ' And how can I help you?'

'You could answer a few questions, sir.'

'Very well.'

Blackstone noticed a Bible on the desk and wondered if Astor would place his hand on it while answering the questions; he didn't.

'Have you any idea why someone was trying to break into your house?'

Astor looked at him as though he were an idiot. He had a point – it was an idiotic question, but there weren't many astute queries to be asked.

Astor said tersely: 'To rob me, I presume.'

'But he must have known that you wouldn't leave any valuables in the house...'

'Valuables? Who said anything about valuables? There could have been money here—'

'But there wasn't?'

'No, as it happens there wasn't.'

'Could he have been after anything other than valuables?' Blackstone asked, watching for any change in expression.

'Such as what?'

'Oh, I don't know. You're in business, Mr Astor, and there must be a lot of information your rivals would like to get their hands on. Ledgers, accounts, building plans...'

'I don't have any rivals,' Astor snapped.

'So you can't throw any light on the motive?'

'No, sir, I can't. And if that's—'

'I was wondering—'

'Yes?' Astor looked at his watch again.

'I was wondering if I could have a look round the house.'

'You can't,' Astor replied. 'Is there anything else?'

'With respect, sir, you don't seem over-anxious to have the thief apprehended.'

'With respect, sir, I doubt your ability to catch him.'

Blackstone said: 'I have the authority of Mr Hays—'

'Mr Hays answers to me.'

'I didn't gain that impression,' Blackstone said.

'You are a very impudent young man.' Astor seemed to soften a little. 'You're from London?'

Blackstone nodded.

'The first place I went to from Germany. I got a job as an oarsman on a timber boat. When I reached London I worked from dawn to dusk – and *tried*' – he almost smiled, reminding Blackstone of Birnie – 'and *tried* to learn English in my spare time. I was there for two years and my worldly goods... worldly goods' – Astor repeated the words, to hear if they sounded right – 'consisted of fifteen guineas and a suit.'

Blackstone said: 'You certainly came up the hard way, sir.'

'I certainly did. And I suspect that you did, too?'

'But not quite as far up as you,' Blackstone murmured, finding to his consternation that he admired the preposterously rich old bastard.

'I booked a passage steerage to Baltimore for five guineas. We were stuck in ice in Chesapeake Bay from January until March. And when I set foot on dry land my...my worldly goods consisted—'

'—of seven flutes and twenty-five dollars...'

Another Birnie-type expression crossed Astor's face. 'I gather you've been reading about me...'

'I've done my homework,' Blackstone told him.

'Good, good...Too few people do these days. That's why I always win. You should go into business,' Astor said, staring hard at Blackstone.

Blackstone shook his head. 'I'm not a businessman.'

'A pity.' Astor banished the possibility from his mind. 'So you know the rest? My first job at two dollars a week with board – beating furs to keep the moths out of them...'

Blackstone said: 'I know a bit about it.'

'Kept my ears and eyes open. That's how I learned the fur trade. That's how I first made money...'

Astor peered at Blackstone and Blackstone wondered whether he was challenging him to raise the Captain Kidd story.

Blackstone said nothing and Astor went on: 'Then, of course, there was the China trade...one ship that visited the Sandwich Islands carried sandalwood to China and made me a hundred thousand dollars. What about that, eh, Blackstone?'

What about it? Was it possible that Astor was trying to explain how he had made a fortune without access to a treasure trove?

'My interests spread from Hudson Bay to Puget Sound to the mouth of the Columbia River. Then, of course, I went in for property ... Don't just look ahead, Blackstone, buy ahead and then build ahead. Keep quiet, keep cool.' He stopped abruptly, having exhausted his favourite topic. Now he was back in the company of a lowly custodian of the law. 'Was there anything else?' He stood up.

'I wanted to look around downstairs. You know, sir, in the area where the break-in was attempted and, perhaps, in the hallway.'

'Very well, you have my permission. But if I find that you've wandered further than the hallway, I'll see to it that Hays claps you in irons.'

Astor escorted Blackstone to the hallway and placed him in the care of the butler, whose predecessor had been sacked for being found drunk in a guest bedroom with the housekeeper on the night of the break-in.

Astor said in his thick accents: 'And don't waste any more of anyone's time asking damn-fool questions. Good-day, Mr Blackstone,' and he was gone.

The butler, who might have been his predecessor's twin, looked at Blackstone with distaste. 'In what way can I help you, sir?'

'I want you to go into the passage where the break-in took place, while I stay here.'

'I don't really think—'

'That's obvious,' Blackstone said. 'So just do what you're told.'

'Now look—'

'No, you look here,' Blackstone snapped. 'Mr Astor made it perfectly plain that you were to co-operate with me.'

The butler went into the passage and Blackstone plunged the key thickly coated with wax into the lock on the front door.

He called out to the butler: 'You can come back now.'

'Is there anything else, *sir*?'

'Yes,' Blackstone said. 'You can get me a drink.'

In fact, Blackstone was able to enter the Astor house sooner than he had anticipated. He met Billy the Bostonian cracksman in the tavern near the Bowery Theatre and got around to discussing the methods of London cracksmen.

During the conversation Blackstone mentioned how slow London locksmiths were in making keys from wax impressions. Billy was surprised. There was no such trouble in New York or Boston, he informed Blackstone – they could come up with a perfectly good key in a few hours. And he named a locksmith who could do just that.

Blackstone frowned. 'Does Hays know about him?'

'Of course he does. But all I've said is that he can make a key in a few hours. He's just good at his trade and old Hays can't fault him for that, now can he?' Billy winked.

Blackstone didn't like accomplices. But this time he had no option. He paid well and within six hours he had a key to Astor's home. Five hours after that, when the Astors were at the theatre, the staff were in the pantry and the watchman hadn't yet come on duty, Blackstone let himself into the house and made straight for the master-bedroom.

On the dressing-table was a jewel case. From his pocket Blackstone produced the smallest of his skeleton keys. A click and the box was open.

Blackstone gazed at the contents and grinned.

CHAPTER TWELVE

The Hall in Hanover Square was packed. Directly beneath the platform, at a long trestle table, sat the newspaper reporters. Behind them affluent New York citizens who had paid a dollar each sat on rows of chairs, and behind them were the less affluent who had paid half the price to stand. At strategic points around the auditorium stood officers, armed with truncheons, enlisted by Hays.

Hays himself stood in the wings of the platform with de Vries and Blackstone. None of them was optimistic about the outcome of the meeting.

'We should have banned it,' de Vries grumbled.

Hays shook his head vehemently and banged his staff. 'Not on your life. We fought the Revolution for freedom and we must allow freedom of speech.'

De Vries turned to Blackstone. 'I hope you will be able to show us how the Bow Street Runners practise crowd control.'

'We don't,' Blackstone replied, taking some snuff. 'It's not one of our duties. We're supposed to catch criminals,' he said, feeling his bruised eye.

Hays said: 'I hear you had an interview with Astor.'

Blackstone nodded. 'He thinks I should go into business.'

De Vries said incredulously: 'You actually met Astor?'

'Aye, crusty old bastard, isn't he.' Blackstone paused, before continuing: 'I put that rumour to him.'

'What rumour?'

'The one about Captain Kidd's treasure.'

'Good grief!' De Vries looked appalled. 'What did he say?'

'He laughed,' Blackstone said. 'At least, I think he did. It was a sort of rusty noise in the back of his throat.'

'I should imagine he did laugh,' Hays said. 'I thought you were supposed to be investigating a crime, not the background of the landlord of New York.'

At the back of the hall the crowd was beginning to shout and stamp. Fanny Campbell was five minutes late for her address on The Liberation of the Female Sex.

A man shouted: 'Come on Fanny, show an ankle.'

There was a lot of laughter and ribald comment. The members of the audience sitting in the chairs turned and regarded the rabble behind them sternly.

'We're going to have trouble,' de Vries said.

'That's what we're here for,' Hays said.

Blackstone said: 'I'll go and see what's happened to her.'

He found her sitting in an ante-room, combing her hair in front of a mirror.

Blackstone said:' Come on, you're late.'

'It's my privilege.' She adjusted a ringlet.

'It's not your privilege to cause a riot.'

'According to you and your cronies out there I'm going to cause one anyway.'

The noise of stamping feet reached the sparsely-furnished room.

Blackstone asked: 'Are you sure you want to go through with it?'

She didn't bother to reply. Instead, she wound a last ringlet round her finger and stood up, speech in hand; a regal figure, like a galleon in full sail, Blackstone thought.

She didn't hesitate in the wings, but strode straight on to the stage, to a raucous reception of cheers and catcalls. At the back of the hall a banner appeared above the heads: THE WOMEN OF NEW YORK DEMAND THAT THE HUSSY FANNY CAMPBELL BE SHIPPED BACK TO ENGLAND. Another blossomed: WELCOME FANNY CAMPBELL – FREE LOVE FOR ALL.

A woman's voice screamed 'Get off the stage you bawdy basket,' and a man shouted 'Let's have some free love now, Fanny'.

The scene reminded Blackstone of a prize-fight. With coloured handkerchieves knotted at their throats, the men standing at the back, passing bottles around, smoking stubby pipes and taking snuff, could have been members of the Fancy. Blackstone took stock of the trouble-makers: a bearded sailor with a barrel chest, swigging from a rum bottle; a bruiser with a broken nose, bawling obscenities; a stout woman with a bleak face and a basketful of rotting fruit. Poor Fanny.

She seemed unperturbed. Waited for the first onslaught of shouting to die down. Raised one hand imperiously. Silence.

She said in ringing tones: 'The men may leave.'

The silence thickened.

Fanny paused before going on: 'I'm talking to the women now. How many times have we been asked – commanded – to leave the room while men talk business? Or whatever it is', she slyly suggested, 'that they talk about when they're alone.'

She held her audience.

She stretched her arms wide. 'Now it is the turn of us women.' A few nervous cheers. 'I say the men *may* leave because, although we seek equal rights, we are still the fair sex and we must retain our dignity.' A pause. 'We must not be churlish, we must not behave like ... men. Therefore I say the men *may* leave. But if they stay' – a conniving smile – 'then they must expect some blunt comments on their attitudes.'

Some female laughter.

De Vries said: 'We could charge her with incitement to violence.'

Hays looked doubtful. 'And play into her hands? Make her a martyr?' He turned to Blackstone. 'What do you think, Mr Bow Street Runner?'

'I think she may win the day,' Blackstone replied, 'although it will be a close thing. It depends whether she can win over the women who are against her. If she does, then the men won't cause trouble. They wouldn't dare,' he grinned.

At the back of the hall the trouble-makers hunched their shoulders, chewed their lips, scowled, spat and waited for a leader to make his presence known.

If there was a leader present, he was forestalled by Fanny Campbell's next ploy – ancient enmities.

She said: 'As you may know, I have just fled from England.'

'Sensible girl,' shouted a man.

She raised one hand in acknowledgement. 'I have thrown off the yoke that you threw off under the leadership of George Washington.'

Even de Vries, Blackstone noted, was mollified. Blackstone thought: the bitch!

Hays asked: 'What do you think of that, Blackie?'

Blackstone grunted.

Fanny went on: 'I have thrown off the yoke of stuffy morality. I have fled from a country where equality is a mockery. Where a woman is still only fit for the kitchen or the drawing-room.'

Blackstone thought she might have mentioned the bedroom, but she was too canny, aware that she would upset the female prudes.

'I have come to the New World, which has been founded on new concepts of freedom, and I am sure that these concepts will be extended to the wives of the soldiers who fought two wars for liberty. To wives, to mothers, to grandmothers and to daughters...'

Scattered applause.

Fanny went on to elaborate her aims: women performing men's jobs – and receiving equal pay; taking part in the administration and government of the city... By now most of the audience was sympathetic, and the meeting might have been a triumph for Fanny if she hadn't been beguiled by the bearded sailor into elaborating on free love.

At the conclusion of her speech he bawled: 'What about free love then?'

'What about it?' Fanny asked.

'You said you were going to talk about free love. This meeting's a fraud and I want my money back.'

The sitting members of the audience turned and hissed. 'Throw him out,' shouted someone. One of Hays's officers edged towards the sailor.

Fanny pointed at the sailor with an accusing finger. 'At no time have I said I would talk about free love. But, as you've raised the question' – Blackstone groaned – 'I will state my views. It has long been the prerogative of the male to seek as many liaisons with women as he wishes, without any stigma attached. In fact, the reverse is true – he is hailed by his fellows as a blade, a dog... Now I ask you, why should there be one set of rules for men and another for women?

Why shouldn't a woman be free to form as many liaisons as she wishes?' She held up both hands to stem the growing agitation in the audience. 'I am not condoning promiscuity, far from it. I am merely stating that women should have as much opportunity in this field as men...'

'Here we go,' Blackstone said to de Vries and Hays. 'She had them eating out of her hand, but now they want to bite it. She's not only upset all the matrons in the audience, but also any husbands who have liaisons outside their marriages...'

The man with the broken nose shouted: 'What about this *field*, darling. Why don't we go there together?'

The bleak-faced woman shouted 'Hussy!' and hurled a rotten pear at the stage.

Two of Hays's men pushed their way through the throng towards the woman. They grabbed her as she threw a tomato and hustled her, screaming and struggling, towards the exit. But another emotion had been kindled in the crowd now – resentment at law and order, authority and discipline.

'Let her go,' screeched another woman. 'It's equal rights, ain't it?' And male voices – 'Let her go, it's Hays's men, get 'em, scrag 'em...'

A bottle crashed down on one of the officers' heads and he disappeared from view.

In the middle of the swells' seats a woman stood up – an elegant lady in grey, who would have graced any vicarage tea party, a doyen of respectability, a dignified upholder of morality. She pointed her parasol at Fanny and shouted: 'Let's tar and feather the bitch.'

Hays said to Blackstone: 'What would the Bow Street Runners do now?'

'Run,' Blackstone said. 'But let's get her off the stage first.'

He ran on to the platform, took Fanny by the arm and tried to propel her towards the ante-room. She tore herself free and said: 'Get your hands off. I can handle this.'

'Don't be stupid,' Blackstone said. 'They're in an ugly mood.'

'So am I,' Fanny said. She addressed the audience again, her tones ringing more stridently than before. 'You're all scared. Scared of progress, as men and women have been throughout history.'

Chairs crashed to the floor and a phalanx of men and women began to head towards the platform. At the back of the hall the fighting had spread: bottles smashed against the walls, cudgels flayed, teeth flew…Blackstone noticed Hays barrelling his way through the brawling mass, laying about him with his staff.

Blackstone made another grab at Fanny, slipped on the spattered remains of the pear and fell.

The mob, headed by the woman in grey, had reached the steps leading to the platform. But the man with the broken nose got to the stage first. He grinned, lunged at Fanny and ripped her gown down the front. She drove her fist into the broken nose and he grinned more fiercely, grabbed her round the waist, pinioning her arms.

De Vries and one of the officers managed to overturn the steps leading to the stage and the advancing mob hesitated. The woman in grey shouted: 'Round the back, we'll get her from the wings.'

Blackstone hit the man with the broken nose in the eye. The man let go of the girl and rounded on Blackstone. They squared up classically, fists held high, and Blackstone was back in his milling days, his yellow colours fluttering from the corner of the ring, trying to tap his opponent's claret, going for the knock-downer, hearing the cries of the Fancy gathered illegally in some green field under a summer sky.

The broken-nosed man feinted with his left, then swung with his right. But Blackstone parried the blow and hit him on the mouth. A little claret, a snarl and an obscenity.

Blackstone heard the sound of a door being battered down. Outraged morality was about to enter from the wings. No time for elegant fisticuffs. Blackstone dodged two ponderous blows, butted broken-nose in the belly and, as he heard the breath whistling out of his lungs, stepped back and hit him in the throat.

As the mob broke down the door, heading for the wings, and as broken-nose slumped gurgling to the floor, Blackstone picked up Fanny and ran in the opposite direction.

She was struggling and clawing. Blackstone slapped her hard across the face. 'Do you want to get killed?'

At the back of the stage he put her down. 'Don't move,' he said, and she didn't. He snatched a pistol from his belt and fired a ball through the lock on a window; the window flew open. He picked her up and bundled her through, then climbed through himself.

The mob was panting behind them. But there was his horse tethered to the fence. As the woman in grey reached the window Blackstone perched Fanny on the horse, mounted behind her, spurred the horse with his heels...

They were away and the free love free-for-all was behind them.

'That's twice you've defied me,' she said.

They were sitting in a field beneath an oak tree.

'Defied you? Rescued would be a better description.'

'You don't understand.' She was unusually quiet.

'I understand perfectly.'

'No.' She nibbled a blade of grass. 'You don't understand because you're a man. You don't understand that all I want to do is to educate women, to restore to them the dignity of their sex.'

'There wasn't much dignity back there.' Blackstone jerked his thumb in the direction of Hanover Square.

'People don't like change. But they'll come round to my way of thinking. Some day...'

'Perhaps if you approached your subject a little more gently... Perhaps if you concentrated less on free love.'

She touched her cheek. 'Did you have to hit me so hard?'

'If I hadn't you'd be dead – or hanging from one of the gas lamps, covered in tar and feathers.'

'I could have handled that lout.'

'He was doing a better job of it.'

'I don't want you interfering any more.'

Blackstone lay on his back and gazed into the cloudless sky. 'Very well, but I'll be a pall bearer at your funeral. In any case, you'd better lie low for a while.'

'What hurts', she said, 'is that it was the women who started it.'

'Ever since Eve,' Blackstone said.

'But why?'

'Because they're scared of what you're telling them. It's been instilled into them over the centuries that they are menials or adornments or targets for male gratification. You're trying to wrench them away from their fixed ideas and they're scared. You know, they're like prisoners who've been so long in jail that the outside world frightens them and they'll do anything to stay in prison. Your trouble', Blackstone told her, 'is that you're before your time.'

'I can't abandon it all,' she said. 'I must go on trying.'

'I thought you would.'

'Are you serious when you say you agree with me?'

'Of course. Why shouldn't women be equal? After all, they have all the pain of producing men ... '

'You astonish me,' she said. 'I should have thought your reactions would have been just the opposite.'

'I grew up with inequality,' Blackstone said.

'You never talk about it much.'

'I was a different person then. It would be like gossiping about a stranger.'

'I wonder—'

'How I would be if I hadn't ... wandered ... over to this side of the law?'

She nodded.

'Much the same, I expect. I can do things and get away with them now because I'm on the right side of the law.'

'And are you ... *doing things* now?'

'I gave you two hundred and fifty dollars,' Blackstone said. 'Remember?'

'That doesn't mean I can't ask you. What are you up to, Blackie?'

'This,' he said, pulling her to him and slipping his hand inside her torn gown.

He could smell newly-mown hay, and the sun was beating down on them, and he longed for a breath of wind. And then it didn't matter any more.

CHAPTER THIRTEEN

For five days Laxton followed Blackstone, and got to know him as well as he knew any man. He admired him and thought he was a worthy adversary, but he didn't fear him.

He decided that Blackstone was probably a patriot. Patriotism wasn't a sentiment with which Laxton was familiar, but he recognised its existence in others. Patriotism, he decided, would be the spur for the duel, not the girl.

He moved to a lodging house overlooking Whitehall Slip and employed a spy in the Eagle Hotel. From the spy he learnt that Blackstone planned to dine at Fraunces' Tavern on the corner of Broad and Pearl Streets. It was an ideal setting for a quarrel based on patriotic conflict, because it was in this tavern, where Francis 'Black Sam' Fraunces had once presided, that Washington had taken leave of his New York officers in 1783, before walking to Whitehall Stairs through a double line of light infantry in blue coats and white breeches and embarking on a barge on his way to retirement at Annapolis.

Laxton also learnt that Blackstone would be dining with the girl Fanny Campbell. This was an advantage, because no man could display cowardice in front of a woman; not that he thought there was any cowardice in Blackstone's character, but he was some sort of policeman and, in other circumstances, he might think it indiscreet to take part in a duel.

From a waiter at Fraunces' Tavern Laxton discovered where Blackstone had booked a table: he booked an adjoining one. Then he returned to his lodgings and selected his guns for the duel – two fine pistols with barrels rifled at the breech. He handled them with love, smiling his snarl at the prospect of the remunerative kill ahead.

They ate venison and drank claret. Blackstone was thoughtful, Fanny subdued. The tavern was crowded, but the jollity of the patrons didn't reach either of them.

Fanny said: 'Things aren't working out for either of us, are they?'

'I've nothing to complain about,' Blackstone said.

'I don't believe you. But I must say it's difficult to catch you in an unguarded moment.'

Blackstone smiled and continued brooding. He had no idea what island Cartier's map depicted; he hadn't located the bulk of Astor's treasure; it was only a matter of time before Astor told Halleck about the visit of the Bow Street Runner and Halleck identified the Runner as the correspondent of *The Times* and they both realised that something was afoot. Blackstone didn't relish the prospect of an interrogation by Hays: he might produce a corpse.

A sallow-faced man in black sat down at the table next to them and ordered venison. He looked as though he needed the nourishment, Blackstone thought.

Fanny sipped her claret and talked about balloons. Blackstone's attention wandered, but he got the gist of her remarks.

She had managed to hire a balloon that had already made a successful ascent from Castle Garden without a passenger. The balloon was a beautiful craft, said to represent the racehorse Eclipse, which had recently been bought by

Walter Livingstone and John Stevens for ten thousand dollars. Fanny had hired the balloon with two hundred of the money Blackstone had given her.

'It's got a knight in armour on top of it,' Fanny said.

'I beg your pardon?'

'You're not listening.'

'You've hired a balloon and it looks like a horse.'

'It doesn't *look* like a horse,' she said, patiently. 'It's merely supposed to represent a horse. It looks like a balloon.'

'I've backed a few horses in my time that have behaved like balloons.'

'You don't take any of this seriously, do you?'

'Yes I do.'

'You don't – but you would if a man was making an ascent.'

'At the best you'll get a ducking in the Hudson and at the worst you'll drown.'

Fanny was silent. Then she leaned across the table and said: 'Listen, this is important to me. I've got to be someone who is admired if I'm going to be successful with my campaign. I've got to prove that I'm equal to any man and the best way to do it – so that everyone can *see* me do it – is to make an ascent in a balloon.'

Blackstone, vaguely aware that the sallow-faced man was staring at them, said: 'It's a risky business.'

'I've got to do it. I've made up my mind.'

'Then you'll do it,' Blackstone said. 'I've learnt that much about you.'

A waiter took away the remains of the venison and placed a bowl of fruit salad on the table. As he walked away, Fanny noticed the sallow-faced man at the next table. She touched Blackstone's arm and whispered: 'That man – have you seen him before?'

Blackstone shook his head. 'Why?'

'He's been following you. I meant to tell you before.'

Blackstone glanced at the man. 'Are you sure?'

'Of course I'm sure. He followed you out of Castle Garden the other day and now he's sitting here beside us.'

'He's not being very subtle about it, is he?'

Fanny said angrily: 'You belittle everything I say.'

Blackstone smiled at her, squeezed her hand, said he was grateful for her concern and helped himself to fruit salad.

They were half-way through the dessert when the sallow-faced man leaned across and said: 'I heard what you said.'

They looked at him in surprise.

Blackstone said: 'What the hell are you talking about?'

'You were making insulting remarks about America and making fun of George Washington.'

Blackstone said: 'I think you'd better be quiet, sir. You appear to be out of your mind.'

'Out of my mind, am I? Well, I'm not deaf and I heard what you said about Washington. I'm surprised you chose the very place where he bid farewell to his officers to insult the name of the greatest man America has ever known.' His voice had risen and people were gazing curiously at the two tables.

'For God's sake be quiet,' Blackstone said.

'I won't be quiet.' The man stood up. 'You lost the war and even now you can't accept defeat. What sort of a man is it that accepts the hospitality of a brave new nation and then insults the host?'

Fanny said: 'You're drunk.'

The sallow-faced man snarled.

The tavern was quiet and there was menace in the air.

Blackstone sighed. 'Just what do you want?'

145

The sallow-faced man thumped the table with his fist. His voice had risen to a shout. 'I say you are a cowardly English swine.'

'Cowardly, am I?'

'Aye, sir, cowardly.'

The room had become a tableau, knives and forks suspended, jaws locked on food.

Blackstone drummed the table with his fingers.

Fanny said: 'Take no notice ... '

Blackstone said: 'That's the most illogical female remark I've ever heard.' He stood up. 'I want everyone here to know that I have at no time insulted your country or its great leader, George Washington.' Disbelief animated a few faces. 'I am English. But I am not a coward.' He turned to the sallow-faced man. 'I have no idea what you're raving about but, in view of your remarks, I have no choice but to call you. You name the time and place and, of course, you have the choice of weapons.'

The sallow-faced man's lip curled. 'Weehawken at dawn – the morning after tomorrow.'

Blackstone shrugged. 'So be it.'

The tableau came to life once more. Excited chatter, fingers pointing ...

Blackstone paid the bill and he and Fanny walked into the gas-lit street. On the way out they passed the captain of the frigate.

Fanny took Blackstone's arm. 'You shouldn't have done it.'

'It's better than being lynched.'

'This isn't an ordinary duel. There's something about that man ... '

'I wonder who put him up to it?'

Fanny held his arm tightly. 'I don't think you should go to Weehawken.'

'You know I've got to.' They headed towards the Eagle. 'Do you think it was the captain who put him up to it?'

'Perhaps.'

'You know,' Blackstone said, thoughtfully, 'I suspect that our sallow-faced friend is a professional duellist.'

'Then he'll kill you.'

'I'm a bit of a professional myself,' Blackstone said, wondering about Birnie's reactions if he heard that one of his Runners, whose duties included the prevention of duels, was participating in one.

They reached the Eagle and Blackstone suggested retiring to his room. But she declined. He offered to ride with her to Greenwich but she shook her head.

Blackstone stared at her perplexed.

'I have things to do,' she said.

And she rode away into the night, handling the horse with the dash and verve of any man.

It was five hours before Fanny Campbell finally returned to Greenwich. She was exhausted, scared for Blackstone, but proud of her accomplishments since leaving the Eagle. She had returned to Fraunces' Tavern and played the sallow-faced man at his own game: she had followed him and now she knew where he lived. She had one more day in which to act.

CHAPTER FOURTEEN

Next day Blackstone collected a blue swallow-tail coat and breeches he had ordered at Brooks Brothers on Catherine Street. He intended to wear them for the duel, reasoning that if he were mortally wounded it would be a shame to leave the new clothes unworn. A bullet and blood would ruin the cloth, but would he care any more?

He spent most of the morning checking his brace of Manton duelling pistols and offering silent praise to Joe Manton, the gunsmith who had brought so many delicate refinements to the weapons used to defend one's honour.

Honour! Blackstone wasn't sure that he had any and still thought that the code of ethics that necessitated two men discharging balls of lead at each other on a ledge overlooking the Hudson at dawn was absurd. In Blackstone's own code an exchange of blows would have sufficed, but his hand had been forced and he knew that an execution rather than a duel had been planned.

In the afternoon he rode to the field where he had been with Fanny, to test his pistols. As he galloped along the dusty road, he wondered: Is this the way it has to end? All those years of brawling life ... green years in the black slums ... the summons to serve on the side of the law and all the soul-searching it entailed. Was it all of such little consequence that its flow could be ended by a single shot?

Blackstone thought of the women he had loved and the men he had sent to the gallows. I would have liked to die in England, he decided, and I would have liked to take a last ride round the Rookery and kiss the girl at the Brown Bear and shake Ruthven by the hand and drink a pot of ale with him.

But mostly Blackstone thought about futility. Was his death predestined for tomorrow? Was it planned and, if so, why had the architect of it all injected so much doubt, so many confused loyalties, into a life that was to be terminated by a bullet on a breathless August morning in New Jersey?

What in God's name was it all about?

The terrible bleakness, not far removed from fear, persevered until Blackstone reached the field. Then he got down to the business of beating his opponent, his would-be assassin, at his own game. And, as he worked, he got to thinking that he might even win the duel, he might survive and there might yet be time to discover the reason for it all.

It is an ancient maxim that the man who knows his guns has an advantage over his opponent. Blackstone set about reviving his knowledge of his two percussion pistols.

He had previously noticed that in the field there was a tree stump with a sturdy branch still attached to it. On to the branch he screwed a vice, and into the jaws of the vice he fitted one of the pistols. He then paced out fourteen yards and put up a target on an artist's easel.

The target was a circular piece of thin wood crisscrossed with lines so that the whole area was covered with diamonds, each an inch wide. The object was to find out the deviation – or throw – of the bullets because, as Blackstone well knew, the pistol had not yet been invented which could fire straight.

Blackstone took off his swallow-tail coat, folded it neatly on the grass and, watched by an inquisitive robin – a large bird bearing no resemblance to the Christmas card robins of England – fired the pistol in the vice at the centre of the target.

The robin flew away and a flock of birds took to the skies from a copse at the end of the field.

Blackstone re-loaded, taking care to use the same quantity of powder, and fired again. Then he examined the target: both balls had fired an inch and a half to the right. The throw was invariably to the right and so Blackstone would fire an inch and a half to the left of his opponent's heart.

He fired one more bullet and it plunged through the hole punched out by the two previous balls. Having ascertained the exact point blank of the first pistol, Blackstone repeated the performance with the second. This time the throw was two inches.

Blackstone unscrewed the second pistol and set about determining how his own aim compared with the precision of the earlier shots fired from the vice. He was not expecting too much because one of his eyes was still bruised and puffy.

He fired each pistol twice. Not bad, he thought, as he examined the bullet holes: they had torn out the centre of the target (the sallow-faced man's heart).

He replaced the pistols in their case, put on his coat and rode back to the Eagle to find two seconds – and a surgeon well versed in extracting bullets from living flesh.

In the lobby he spoke to two young men – a lawyer and an accountant – who agreed to act for him; agreed, Blackstone thought, with unseemly enthusiasm. They promised to bring a doctor who was no stranger to Weehawken.

Blackstone had once read a book about the way a duel-list should behave on and off the field. The author favoured theatrical nonchalance – a bottle of Madeira, a decent cigar and perhaps a game of chess on the eve of the duel, then early to bed with some light reading; an early call to ensure that he arrived at the rendezvous on time – prefer-ably before his opponent; a meagre breakfast such as tea and biscuits and maybe a small measure of diluted brandy before the hostilities 'if he was of a nervous disposition'.

Blackstone had other ideas about his eve-of-duel behav-iour and he certainly didn't favour light reading. If these were to be his last hours on earth, then he preferred some-thing more substantial in his bed.

With this in mind he rode to Greenwich in search of Fanny. But she wasn't there, and hadn't been there all day, he was told.

Bitterly, he returned to the Eagle where he ate a lobster washed down with a bottle of Sauterne. He put in his early call, went to bed and dreamed that he was twelve years old and standing on the scaffold outside Newgate.

While Blackstone was riding to Greenwich to find her, Fanny was keeping surveillance on Laxton's lodging house.

She sat in a coffee house across the street, waiting for him to leave. She sat there from 6 p.m. till 8 p.m., attracting considerable attention and dismissing two potential suitors with vigour.

At 8.05 she saw Laxton – whose name she had learnt from the manager of the lodging house, for two dollars – leave and walk in the direction of the Battery. He walked slowly, head bowed, and Fanny realised that his slight build gave him an advantage over Blackstone, because his target area was that much smaller.

She watched until he turned a corner, then allowed another five minutes to elapse in case he returned. She was scared for Blackstone and the intensity of her fear surprised her. She suspected that she was in love with the Bow Street Runner and wasn't sure why. Perhaps he was the sort of man with whom she wanted to be equal. There were unknown depths to the man and his physical attraction, she decided, had assumed a new significance when he had displayed understanding of what she was trying to achieve.

A hard man, an arrogant man, a masculine man – and a compassionate man. Please God don't let him die. Fanny paid for her coffee and went about the business of aiding and abetting God…

The lodging house was of the type where a strange woman wandering the corridors was not exceptional. She had obtained a duplicate key from the manager and, within a couple of minutes, was inside Laxton's room.

It was a seedy cubicle, sparsely furnished, walls spattered with the squashed remains of insects. Fanny found what she was looking for in the wardrobe.

Ten minutes later she was riding back to Greenwich. She thought about calling at the Eagle but no, whatever happened at dawn tomorrow, Blackstone would need a good night's sleep. Which was regrettable because more than anything she needed his arms around her and the sound of his heartbeat in her ear.

In another part of town Fitz-Greene Halleck pensively poured himself a glass of port from a cut-glass decanter. So the correspondent of *The Times* was, in fact, Blackstone the Bow Street Runner. He smiled at the rich old man sitting at the other side of the table and said: 'I don't think he will be running very much further.'

The old man didn't reply: he picked up a glass of iced water and drank it thirstily as though it were champagne.

And in a bawdy house near McKibben and Cayley, the grocers on South Street, Laxton did what he always did on the eve of a duel. And, as always, he was peculiarly submissive with the girl – submissive, that is, for a man with fifteen lives to his credit and the probability of a sixteenth notch on his pistol at dawn the next day.

Chapter Fifteen

The duelling ground was below the heights of Weehawken, a mere ledge a few yards wide, about twelve yards long, perched twenty feet above the Hudson.

Blackstone arrived by boat while the new day was still a green glow on the skyline. With him were his seconds, one slightly drunk, and the surgeon, who was completely drunk and had been singing songs from the War of Independence while they crossed the river.

The second who was sober, the lawyer, told Blackstone: 'Don't worry, he always rises to the occasion, however lush he is.'

As the light grew stronger Blackstone examined the duelling ground. It was his prerogative as the challenger to choose the distance: he would choose fourteen yards, the distance at which he had ascertained the throw of his pistols. This was his advantage and he hoped his opponent had judged his own deviation at a different distance; not, Blackstone thought, that it would make much difference – the man was a professional and would have tested the accuracy of his guns at many distances. Doubtless his pistols also had rifling near the breech.

Blackstone decided that firing should be 'at mutual pleasure', not regulated. And, as the slander had been a gross one, he would demand that the seconds supply two pistols instead of one.

Blackstone asked the lawyer if he knew how much powder to pour into each pistol.

The lawyer nodded. 'The equivalent of seven percussion caps.'

'You seem to know your business,' Blackstone said.

'I should – I've acted in six duels already.'

'And how did your men fare?'

'They all lost,' the lawyer said.

Blackstone stared across the broad river to the lights of Manhattan. He would like to have been on the banks of the Thames; he would like to have spent the last hours with Fanny... Why had she failed him? As the stars faded his soul was bleak. Beneath him a yacht sidled through the calm water, an anchor splashed. Then a rowboat came skimming up to the shore and four men alighted – his opponent had arrived.

The sallow-faced man nodded at Blackstone and went about his business as methodically as an executioner. He took off a black cloak and laid it on the ground; the seconds conferred; Blackstone drank his tumbler of diluted brandy, remembering similar scenes on the duelling grounds of London, where it had been his duty to break up the assembly and cart the duellists off to Bow Street.

Blackstone glanced at his opponent's seconds to see if they looked the sort who would *accidentally* fire another shot if the sallow-faced man's bullet missed the target. One of them did: he was the captain of the frigate.

The captain bowed low and Blackstone returned the bow.

The antagonists took up their positions beneath the fading scimitar of the moon. Blackstone's doctor sat up and looked around, apparently doubtful as to where he was. The seconds handed each man a pistol.

The stage was set, but the performance was immediately flawed.

The sallow-faced man shouted: 'This isn't my pistol!' And, grabbing the captain of the frigate, he snatched the second pistol and shouted again: 'Nor is this. I've been tricked ... I can't shoot.'

The captain examined the pistols. 'What the devil are you talking about? You brought the guns from your room this morning.'

'They are not my guns.' Fear nipped at the sallow-faced man's words.

The other second, a fat man with pox scars on his face, rammed the butt of one pistol into Laxton's belly. 'Here, take hold of this – they're your barkers and you damn well know it.'

Blackstone held up his hand and walked over to the group. 'What is your name, sir?'

'You've tricked me, duped me.'

'Not me. I ask you again – what is your name?'

'His name is Laxton,' the fat man said.

'And his first name?'

'Charles,' the second replied.

Blackstone pointed at the silver plates on the butts of the pistols. On each were the initials C.L. 'What does the C. stand for then? Charlotte, Christine, Charmaine ...?'

The captain of the frigate turned snarling on the sallow-faced man. 'For God's sake what are you playing at? You accused this man – pointing at Blackstone – 'of being a coward. Now you're behaving like a snivelling coward yourself. Perhaps, sir, you would like to swoon away ...'

Blackstone said to the captain: 'Perhaps, sir, you would like to take his guns?'

The surgeon sat down and began to sing.

Gulls flew low over the ledge, the sun rose, the heat began to grow.

Laxton said quietly: 'They are not my guns. On my oath, they are not my guns.'

'If you wish you may apologise', Blackstone said, 'and that will be the end of the matter.'

Laxton stared at him for a few seconds before whispering: 'No, sir, I am a match for you with a toy pistol loaded with a cork.' And Blackstone realised with surprise that, although the man was probably a cheat, he wasn't a coward.

Blackstone wondered if he should postpone the encounter. But no, he would then be the coward, and the pistols must belong to Laxton because they had been taken from his room and there were the initials C.L. on the butts. Was it some sort of trick to unnerve him?

Blackstone said: 'Very well, let us take our places.'

The lawyer handed Blackstone first one pistol, then the other. The captain of the frigate did likewise with Laxton's pistols.

Blackstone adopted the firing posture. Sideways to narrow the target area, right arm holding the pistol to shield as much of the body as possible, feet close together.

An inch and a half to the left of Laxton's heart...

Laxton fired first.

Blackstone didn't have to bother.

The pistol in Laxton's hand exploded in a blast of flying metal. Part of the barrel tore a hole in his chest, fragments of metal shredded his face. He fell to the ground, blood pumping from the wound in his chest.

When Blackstone reached him he was dead, what was left of his mouth twisted in a snarl.

The captain of the frigate lay on the ground, blood seeping from a wound in his leg.

Later Blackstone, his seconds and his surgeon rowed back to the Battery. As they passed the yacht that had anchored at dawn, Blackstone thought he recognised a man standing on the deck. An old man with canny features. But he wasn't sure.

He didn't meet her till the evening. They walked on the Battery, listening to the music from Castle Garden and, when it grew dark, watching fireworks from the Garden daub the sky red, green and gold.

Blackstone was still a little stunned. I am alive and Laxton is dead, he thought, and neither of us had any part in it. But who did?

He asked: 'Where were you last night?'

'I didn't feel too well.'

'I could have been killed this morning.'

She took his arm. 'But you weren't.' She paused. 'Did you want me with you?'

'Of course. The condemned man's last wish ... '

'I'm glad,' she said.

'But you weren't there ... '

A steamship, its decks ablaze with light, nosed its way through the motionless sails on its way to Steam Boat Wharf; a rocket – representing a dove laying myriad coloured eggs, according to the programme – exploded over the bay and laid its clutch.

Blackstone waited till the colours had dissolved and then said: 'You seem to have made a remarkable recovery. What was it – the vapours?'

'I'm sorry I wasn't with you,' she said.

'So am I.'

They leaned on the wooden fence and gazed out across the bay. 'What exactly happened over there?' she asked. 'You haven't told me much.'

'There isn't much to tell. A man was murdered.'

'But it was a duel...'

'I told you, Laxton's pistol exploded. It sometimes happens if too much powder is used...but Laxton was too old a hand to let that happen. Besides, he claimed that they weren't his pistols.'

'But they must have been...'

'Perhaps. God only knows. I've been accused of tampering with them.'

Fanny said: 'The man was a professional assassin. He would have killed you – his guns would have been prepared so that you didn't have a chance. He was a murderer, he was murdered.'

'It wasn't a fair fight,' Blackstone said. 'I was accused of being a coward. Now it looks as though I arranged his death in a peculiarly cowardly way.'

'But who arranged the duel? Who hired him?'

Blackstone shrugged. 'The sea captain maybe. Or your friend Halleck, financial adviser to John Jacob Astor.'

'But why? Why should he want to kill you? You see, Blackie, you haven't told me what you're up to.'

'Maybe I would have last night, but you weren't there.'

'I am now.'

'Too late,' Blackstone said, tersely.

'Could anything else have made his pistol explode? I mean anything else except too much powder?'

'A dozen things,' Blackstone said. 'A man who understands guns could easily have fixed the pistols so that they exploded at the first spark.'

'And you think that's what happened?'

'I can't think of anything else. You see, the pistols had Laxton's initials on them, so they must have belonged to him. If I had thought they didn't belong to him, I wouldn't have gone through with it. A man is entitled to have his own guns when he faces death—'

'Even doctored guns?'

'What makes you think they were doctored?' Blackstone turned and stared at Fanny. 'You seem to know a lot about duelling pistols. How could they be doctored?'

'I don't know,' she said vaguely. 'I seem to remember reading something about rifling in the barrels.'

'Strange reading for a lady!'

'I don't confine myself to penny romances.'

They turned and walked back towards Castle Garden, where a firework was spraying golden rain into the air. Couples strolled around them and everyone gave the impression that they were waiting for rain, or for a breeze.

Blackstone asked: 'Where did you go when you felt…indisposed?'

'Back to Greenwich,' she told him.

Blackstone was silent for a moment before remarking: 'You weren't there when I came looking for you.'

'I didn't know—'

He gripped her arm with his hand. 'Where were you?'

'You're hurting me,' she said.

'Where were you?'

'It's none of your business.'

'I suspect it is.'

'I was with a friend.'

'Halleck?'

'I don't have to tell you where I was.'

Blackstone said quietly: 'You tampered with those pistols, didn't you?'

'Don't be stupid,' she said. 'What would I know about pistols?'

'You seem to know quite a lot about balloons and that's hardly a ladylike pursuit.'

'I can assure you I know very little about guns.'

'I believe you,' Blackstone said, thoughtfully. 'Someone must have helped you. Who? Tell me who before I take you round to see Hays.'

They sat down on a bench. Blackstone took some snuff and waited.

'Very well,' she said, after a while. 'It was me. I didn't want you murdered.'

'You tampered with those pistols?' Blackstone said, incredulously.

'No. I went to a gunsmith. He sold me a brace of duelling pistols with all the refinements—'

'But the initials…' Blackstone interrupted.

'A silversmith inscribed those for me. Then all I had to do was wait for Laxton to leave his lodgings and substitute the pistols.'

'And the pistols – were they tampered with?'

Fanny Campbell didn't reply.

'The guns – were they doctored?'

'Yes,' she said, softly. 'The gunsmith fixed them. I don't know what he did, but he said they would explode when fired.' She put her arms round Blackstone, holding him tight. 'I did it for you, Blackie – I didn't want you to be killed.'

Blackstone pushed her away. 'I can fight my own battles.'

'So can I… But you always fight them for me.'

'You realise you murdered a man?'

'I prevented an execution.'

'Your logic', Blackstone said, coldly, 'has always amazed me.'

'But we're together now—'

'Do you realise that I 'm branded a coward in New York?'

'Is that so important?'

'Yes,' Blackstone said. 'It's very important.' It was a question of honour and that's what they had been duelling about, even if he didn't understand it. Yes, it was very important. 'You meddled and you fought my duel for me in the most cowardly way and you killed a man.' Blackstone stood up. 'What you don't seem to realise is that I might have won the duel. That's the worst part of it.'

He walked away, leaving her sitting alone on the bench.

Chapter Sixteen

Hays read the newspapers with mounting anger.

The crime rate soaring in the gas-lit streets... reports of bathing *au naturel* – couldn't they come out with it and say nude – in the East River... a woman strangled in the community of Bloomingdale... the first passenger railroad train to be pulled by horse on the Baltimore and Ohio line... a duellist named Charles Laxton killed by an exploding pistol at Weehawken across the Hudson...

And who was his opponent? Edmund Blackstone, Bow Street Runner.

The iniquity of the affair outraged Hays. Blackstone – his guest – was the man dispatched from England to help control the increase in crime. What happened? Crime continued to increase and Blackstone participated in a duel – a practice which Bow Street was committed to stamping out – and a particularly unsavoury affair into the bargain.

It seemed that the strapping Englishman who had been a guest at his home hadn't even fought fairly, had doctored Laxton's guns so that the first pressure on the hair-spring trigger blew the pistol into lethal chunks of metal.

What's more, there appeared to be a strong possibility that Blackstone, currently investigating the burglary at Astor's house, was in fact the culprit. Blackstone investigating Blackstone! The man was a rogue. Why had Sir Richard

Birnie sent him? Because I asked for him, Hays reflected ruefully; because de Vries had said he was a good man.

And the girl with whom Blackstone was consorting – she too was trouble. She had been allowed to make her speech and the result was a full-scale riot. She had escaped, of course, with Edmund Blackstone.

And the newspapers were now mounting a campaign against the High Constable. Why had he permitted the speech to take place? What steps was he taking to control the activities of footpads?

What indeed? He had sought the guidance of a Bow Street Runner who had probably broken into the home of New York's richest landlord and then participated in a gory mockery of a duel at Weehawken.

It would be interesting, Hays mused, stroking his formidable nose, to know who had hired Laxton, a notorious professional duellist. He cracked his staff across his desk and a clerk, always alert to such a summons, appeared in the doorway.

Hays said: 'Bring in the English captain.'

The captain of the frigate limped into Hays' office, sat down opposite him and said: 'I demand to know why I am being kept here.'

'It should be perfectly obvious,' Hays remarked. 'You were aiding and abetting a duel. As you may know, a gentleman named Aaron Burr was disfranchised by the laws of New York for having fought a duel, and was charged with murder in New Jersey.'

'Does your jurisdiction extend to New Jersey?'

'That needn't concern you,' Hays snapped, his dislike for the smooth-faced Englishman increasing; at least you had to respect Blackstone for his outrageous behaviour, but not this popinjay who wasn't even wearing his uniform. God knows it wouldn't have suited him. 'Your ship is in the port of New York and New York *is* in my jurisdiction.'

'I demand to be released,' the captain said.

'But you are not being held, sir.'

'Then—' The captain stood up, turned, yelped as Hays' staff cracked across the desk and sat down again as Hays said: 'You'll leave when I permit it, sir.'

'But—'

'When I permit it!'

'The King shall hear of this,' the captain said.

'You forget', Hays said, 'that we no longer owe allegiance to your King. And, from what I hear of him, we are fortunate to be in that situation ... '

'I demand—'

'You demand nothing, sir. It is I who do the demanding. I am not one of your miserable crew existing on maggot-infested meat and mouldering biscuits while you eat off the fat of the sea at the captain's table.' Hays leaned across the desk. 'Now look here, captain, there are one or two points I want to clear up before I write to your King, questioning the behaviour of a captain of His Majesty's Navy who thinks fit to act as second to a professional duellist.'

'You wouldn't—'

'Oh yes I would,' Hays said, with satisfaction. 'Unless, of course, you agree to co-operate ... '

'Very well,' said the captain, fear quivering in his voice.

Hays asked him why he was acting as second to a man who wanted to kill a fellow Englishman. Surely he should have been Blackstone's second? Hays was surprised at the vehemence of the captain's reaction.

The captain said:'I wanted to see him dispatched to hell.'

Hays raised his eyebrows. 'Strong language.'

'He is a swine—'

'Not such a bad animal – we have a lot of them in Manhattan—'

'—and he deserved to die.'

Hays said: 'Perhaps you would explain the…ah…intensity of your feelings.'

'He forced his attentions on a young lady on board my ship.'

'Miss Campbell?'

'Exactly. A sweet, innocent young lady—'

'As sweet and innocent as an amorous alley-cat—'

'I shall have to call you, sir!'

Hays raised his hand. 'Calm down, captain. We can't have the High Constable participating in a duel, now can we?' Not, Hays thought, that you would have the guts to fight a duel – accomplice to a hired assassin is more your mark, my son. 'Very well, Blackstone forced his attentions upon the innocent and defenceless Miss Campbell. What happened then?'

'She came running to me for help and I was forced to lay Blackstone out.'

'Blackstone the Blackguard, eh?'

'Your words, sir.'

'Aye, my words,' said Hays, knowing from past experience of interrogation that the reverse of what the captain had related was the truth. 'So at least I have an idea about your…involvement. Now tell me this, captain, who was employing Laxton?'

'Employing him?'

'Aye, employing him. You aren't hard of hearing, are you captain?'

'I didn't know anyone was employing him. All I can tell you is that he accused Blackstone of being a coward and Blackstone had to call him.'

'And you volunteered to act as second?'

'Someone had to represent Laxton.'

'From what I hear,' Hays remarked, 'he wouldn't have been short of seconds – he's been doing this sort of thing for years. Did he just *happen* to ask you?'

The captain fingered his calf where the blood showed through his breeches. 'As it happens, I was just entering the tavern after Blackstone had called Laxton.'

'And you offered your services?'

'Why not?'

'It seems odd, that's all, an Englishman offering his services against an Englishman…'

'I've already told you—'

'So you have,' Hays murmured. 'So you have. Didn't it occur to you that Laxton had deliberately provoked the quarrel?'

'No, sir, it did not.'

'And what, may I ask, were you doing at the tavern?'

'I went there for a meal and a glass of ale because my ship is becalmed in your damned harbour.'

'I'm sorry about the lack of wind,' Hays observed. And, staring hard at the captain, hand grasping the staff: 'Are you sure you weren't following Blackstone?'

'Following him? Why the devil should I be?'

'I don't know.' Hays brooded. 'It was just a thought. Perhaps whatever happened on your frigate still rankles…After all, Blackstone was attacked quite recently…'

'Are you suggesting—'

'Merely following a line of thought…Did you hire foot-pads to attack Blackstone, captain?'

'I did not.'

'I wonder who did,' Hays mused. And then: 'Are you sure you don't know who hired Laxton?'

'I didn't know he *was* hired.'

'You may rest assured, sir, that he was. Laxton would only embark upon a duel if the pay was sufficient. You see it was his job – and he was damn good at it ... until someone tampered with his guns. Or substituted another brace,' Hays added, thoughtfully.

The captain said: 'Will that be all?'

'I think so,' Hays said, 'for the time being. Judging by the look of the sky you won't be leaving New York for a few days.'

Hays rapped the desk with his staff and said to the clerk: 'Get de Vries and tell him I want Blackstone found and brought here.' He instantly regretted the timing of the order because of the pleasure that creased the captain's smooth cheeks.

Half an hour later two of Hays's men called at the Eagle Hotel. They were told by the manager that Blackstone had booked out of the hotel earlier that day. Where had he gone? The manager shrugged. 'He didn't say. But', he added, 'he paid all his bills.' It seemed to surprise him.

In fact, Blackstone had moved to a room in State Street, beside the Battery, with a balcony overlooking the bay. It was an elegant house, like all those in State Street, and such was its aura of gentility that it seemed unlikely that anyone would go there seeking a man on the run.

Because that's what I am, Blackstone thought, taking off his boots and lying on the bed in the high-ceilinged room. I was the hunter, now I'm the hunted.

He hadn't the slightest doubt that Hays would be after him, as Birnie would be after his quarry in similar circumstances in London. It had been a disastrous sequence of events from the moment he had left England. He had been attacked, betrayed by a woman – she had doubtless acted in his interests, but that was immaterial – failed to find the bulk of Kidd's treasure and was the proud owner of a meaningless map.

Outside, seagulls perched on the impotent sailing boats and cried about loneliness.

I suppose, Blackstone thought, Fanny did try to save my life – possibly *did* save my life. But a woman doesn't fight a man's battles for him...

The map. He took it from his pocket and studied it once more. Where? It could be in the Indian Ocean, it could be in the Mediterranean...

Should he catch the next packet to England? He liked New York, but the feeling hadn't been reciprocated.

He swung his legs off the bed and sat gazing over blue water. What would I do in Hays's case? Interrogate the captain of the frigate, of course, because he was the missing link, the man who probably knew who had hired Laxton.

And when Hays has finished with the captain I shall interview him, Blackstone decided. But not as a Bow Street Runner, nor as a correspondent of *The Times*.

Blackstone waited till dusk. Then he memorised the map for the last time, burnt it, and slipped out of the fine house in the fashionable street, in search of a disguise that was neither fine nor fashionable.

Chapter Seventeen

The man pushing the wheelbarrow with the charcoal furnace cried: 'Hot corn! Hot corn! Come and buy your piping hot corn!'

The captain of the frigate, limping along Broad Street, decided the corn-seller was mad. Who would want piping hot corn on yet another stinking hot night?

The captain enjoyed New York, but he preferred it in winter. He had been to the city once before – in 1821, when you could walk across the ice to Brooklyn and Governor's Island – and he longed for the muffled quiet of snow, for its bluish glow in his bedroom at dawn.

In fact, the captain was homesick. He was, he acknowledged, a very ordinary specimen of manhood; it was his birthright and it wasn't his fault. But his mediocrity had been complicated by wealth, by a father who wanted a seadog for a son. It had taken the captain years to conquer sea-sickness; he had never conquered his cowardice.

It was, the captain reflected, a pestilence that so many of the qualities he had inherited through no fault of his own were condemned by society. Why? What was more natural than cowardice? Why get hurt when there were alternatives? Why put yourself in the way of a bullet when it was more prudent to hide behind the flesh of the foolhardy?

Nevertheless the captain did envy in others the qualities he didn't possess – courage, confidence, swagger and virility. Which was why he hated Blackstone, the hatred being the most powerful emotion he had ever experienced.

The captain had always believed that a smooth, sophisticated approach with women more than compensated for bristling self-assurance. Why not? It was only the fault of the authors of romance and adventure stories that crude masculinity had been allowed to supplant more cultivated approaches.

And he had been on the point of proving his point – with a token struggle from the girl – when Blackstone had burst into the cabin.

Blackstone!

Why had he had the misfortune of being ordered to take the blackguard on board? The man was notorious in London and yet there he had been, sitting at the captain's own table, flirting with the only woman on board.

The bitch!

The captain turned into a tavern near Pine Street. He ordered a brandy and sat down at a table, his wounded leg outstretched, blood dark and stiff on his white breeches.

The bitch! The captain no longer deluded himself that she preferred subtlety to conventional virility. Because she was an anomaly among her sex, a woman seeking equality with men, and in Blackstone she had found the perfect antagonist.

He sipped the brandy and felt it stoke the fires of hatred. With Blackstone out of the way he could have reassembled his forces and made another approach to Fanny Campbell. Which was why he had hired the footpads.

Once again he had been thwarted, and then he had been given the opportunity of a ring-side view of Blackstone's demise on the ledge beneath Weehawken heights. Again a fiasco.

Pain jabbed the captain's leg. Why had Hays been so insistent that Laxton had been employed to kill Blackstone? What the hell was Blackstone's game in New York? The captain ordered another brandy; the pain subsided to a throbbing ache, like a bad tooth stupefied by alcohol.

But I'll get him, the captain decided on his third brandy. I have time – until a breeze ruffles the sails in the bay.

He left the tavern, walked down Pine Street into Broadway, turning left towards Bowling Green. The gaslight was pale and bright, a contradiction of the steamy night.

The hunchback materialised from a side street. He was ragged and dirty, but he had wares to sell and, the captain reasoned, the wares were possibly cleaner. Nevertheless he made a token gesture – 'Get out of my way,' he said, waving his arm.

'Very pretty girls,' said the hunchback. 'Very experienced.'

'I said get out of my way.'

'I see you're limping, sir.'

'What of it?'

'Very gentle these girls... They won't hurt your leg... they'll bathe it and bandage it and then—'

'Then what?' the captain asked, despite himself.

The hunchback spread wide his arms. 'Whatever you please.'

The captain hesitated. The brandy had muddled his reason. He asked: 'How much?' and was surprised at himself.

'It depends... on what you want... on who you want... '

'A dollar?'

'Maybe... maybe a little more.'

'Where is it?'

'Just round the corner,' said the hunchback, who had a curious drawl. Perhaps he was from the South.

'I'll take a look.'

The hunchback smiled. 'Just as you please.'

They went down a dark lane, leaving the gaslight flaring behind them. Dogs slunk away and a hog trotted past. The captain thought he heard footsteps behind, but he wasn't sure. But they had gone far enough and he said to the hunchback: 'I'm going back.'

The hunchback pointed at a house a little further on. There were candles in one window. 'That's where the girls are,' the hunchback murmured. 'Very beautiful girls... you will enjoy their company.'

The brandy was still warm inside him and the captain said: 'Very well, but they'd better be good.'

They walked on. Behind them a noise? The captain swung round. Nothing but the gaslight in the background.

'In here,' the hunchback said. They turned into a path leading to the house. The hunchback opened the door and ushered the captain inside.

The room was empty and two candles burned at the window.

'What the hell...' The captain rounded on the hunchback.

But the hunchback was now six feet two inches tall. Blackstone said: 'You and me must have a little talk, captain.' He removed a pillow from the back of his ragged jacket and stretched.

Fear lurked inside the captain, but this time its companion was hatred. He hated this man more than he had ever hated anyone. He lunged with his left fist, but the blow was parried and Blackstone's right fist cracked into the side of his head. He fell down.

Blackstone said: 'You might as well answer my questions down there.'

'One of these days', the captain said, 'I'll see you hung, drawn and quartered.'

'You nearly saw me shot, didn't you, captain.'

'Aye, except that you doctored Laxton's guns.' The captain stood up.

Anger rasped in Blackstone's voice. 'I didn't tamper with those pistols.'

'Who did – Laxton?'

'They weren't his pistols.'

'Whose were they then?' Again the captain was surprising himself: courage in the face of the enemy.

'They were substituted by someone who wanted him dead.'

'They had his initials on them.'

'Aye, common enough initials.' Blackstone leaned against the wall, reaching for his snuff box. 'But I haven't brought you here to discuss the details of Laxton's death. I want to know who hired him.'

'I don't know,' the captain said. 'Hays asked me that and I told him the same.'

'You'd better tell me something else. When someone sets out to murder me I like to know who. Was it you?'

The captain shook his head.

'But you put those footpads on to me, eh, captain?'

'I did not.' But there was a change in his tone: the ring of truth was cracked.

Blackstone said: 'I don't want to hurt you. You're lying about the footpads, but that doesn't matter. I want to know who hired a professional killer to finish me off. And I want to know why. And you are going to tell me.'

The captain made a bolt for the door and tripped over Blackstone's outstretched foot. He fell, picked himself up again.

'Who hired Laxton?'

'I don't know.'

The door was kicked open from outside. 'No more he does,' said de Vries, pointing at Blackstone and telling two members of the Watch: 'Seize that man and hold him hard – he's dangerous.'

CHAPTER EIGHTEEN

In the field where Fanny Campbell and Edmund Blackstone had once lain in the sun together the great balloon strained at its moorings.

Its multicoloured skin was dimpled despite the lack of wind and the ropes holding it sawed at the trees to which they were tied. Beneath the balloon hung a basket large enough to hold three people.

Seated on horseback, Fanny gazed with mixed feelings at the balloon that, later in the afternoon, would lift her into the sky. How far up would it go? And in what direction? According to the experts – none of whom had made an ascent – it was perfectly safe: there was no sign of wind and the descent could be easily controlled by expelling the gas.

If balloon navigation was so simple, why had Madame Johnson, who had made her ascent from Castle Garden, landed in a pond on Long Island?

It was 9 a.m. on another fine late summer morning and no one believed in autumn or winter any more. Fanny was due to make her ascent at 3.30 and already crowds were beginning to assemble. A disciple of free love projecting herself into the heavens! What more could you wish for?

But one person would be missing at 3.30 – or so Fanny feared. Blackstone had been missing for two days and she didn't think there was any chance that he would make an appearance. Why should he? In the circumstances her attitude would be the same.

Fanny touched the horse with her heels and they cantered back towards Manhattan Toe.

She had interfered and fought his battle for him, fought it like a coward, and her reactions would have been the same if Blackstone had meddled with a duel she was fighting. But I would do the same again, she thought, as she rode along Greenwich Street, past Liberty and Cedar Streets. I would do anything, however shabby, to save the life of the man I love.

But where was Blackstone? Laxton had been murdered and Blackstone was a fugitive. Assuming that he had been taken prisoner, she had visited Hays and confessed that she had substituted doctored weapons for Laxton's guns.

Hays had stared at her with grim disbelief. 'In the first place,' he had said, 'I have no idea where your precious Bow Street Runner is.'

'You haven't caught him?'

'No, ma'am. But if I do, then I shall put him on the first ship back to England and I shall request Sir Richard Birnie to take action against him.' Hays had reached instinctively for the staff lying on his desk. 'He has taken advantage of my hospitality, he has betrayed my trust. I should never have trusted a lawman who carries guns,' he added.

Fanny said: 'But he didn't do it. I swear it – I changed Laxton's guns.'

'Prove it,' Hays said. 'Where are Laxton's pistols?'

Fanny told Hays that she had thrown them in the Hudson and Hays said: 'So what do you want me to do, dredge the river?'

'I'll take you to the gunsmith who sold me the doctored pistols.'

And so they had gone to the gunsmith, who had denied ever seeing Fanny. And then to the silversmith, who had been equally vehement in his denials.

Outside the silversmith Hays said: 'But I must say I admire your loyalty, Miss Campbell.'

'It's the truth, I tell you.'

'Why would you do such a thing? Blackstone seems to be quite capable of taking care of himself.'

'Not against a professional assassin.'

'A professional against a professional. I should say they were equally matched. But I would give a year's pay to know who hired Laxton ... and why it was so important for someone to have Blackstone killed.' He began to walk back towards his office. 'Has it occurred to you that they may have succeeded?'

'Yes,' Fanny said softly, 'it has.'

Now, riding towards the Battery, Fanny Campbell decided to make a last bid to find Blackstone. A last bid because the ascent in the balloon had an air of finality about it, the climax of the past few weeks. If Blackstone didn't materialise before the balloon went up, then she would know he was dead.

She inquired again at the Eagle, but no one had seen him since he had paid his bill. She visited the taverns that he frequented; no one had seen the big Englishman who had blown Laxton off the face of the earth.

Billy the Boston cracksman bought her a drink. 'Sweet on him, are you?' he asked.

'I suppose so.'

'Understandable,' he said, as they sat down at a table. 'He must be an attractive man to women.'

'Can you help me?'

The burglar examined the diamond rings on his fingers. 'I could make some inquiries. I've got contacts who wouldn't give the time of day to Hays or his men.'

'Then help me, Billy,' she said.

'And if he's dead?'

'Then there's nothing any of us can do.'

'Then perhaps in time we might walk out together?'

She looked at him in surprise. 'In time, perhaps,' she lied.

'Ah, but you don't mean that, do you? You wouldn't be the woman I think you are if you did... But there's nothing wrong with hoping, now is there?'

She smiled at him. 'You're a good man, Billy.'

'Never say that,' the cracksman replied, 'or you'll ruin my reputation. I've just had a bit of success in Boston,' he went on, ordering two brandies from the waiter. 'They caught one of my men and put him inside. But he didn't stay there long. Four horses, grappling-irons and we had the bars off his cell in the time it takes to swallow a brandy.' He drank his brandy in one gulp.

'So you'll help?'

'Of course. I've got a couple of mates on the Watch at the moment. They might know a thing or two. You see, I'm thinking of starting up here in New York. Money's pouring into the place like flood water. Soon it'll be the richest city in the world...' He paused. 'I hear you're going up in a balloon this afternoon?'

She nodded.

'I'll be there. And when you come down I might have some news for you. But don't raise your hopes too high.'

She thanked him and went outside into the hot street and gazed up at the blue sky into which she would shortly be voyaging.

Blackstone couldn't see the sky. Hadn't seen it for two days.

He was ravenously hungry, desperately thirsty and his body ached from the beating handed out by de Vries and one of his men.

He wasn't sure where he was, but he could hear steam ships hooting and seagulls crying. He could smell decay and vermin and he could feel pain. That was all.

He estimated that de Vries and one of his henchmen came to him about every six hours. The questions were always the same, the methods of interrogation varying little – fists and boots and starvation, thirst occasionally slaked by a few mouthfuls of water, because they didn't want him to die. Not yet.

In Blackstone's book they were amateurs at extracting information. The first beating had been the worst; after that the fists and boots merely sank into the cushions of pain.

Sitting against a wall running with water, opposite a barred window, his wrists and ankles bound with thick nautical rope, Blackstone thought about the first interrogation.

Ironically the questions had provided Blackstone with the answers for which he had been searching. Or most of them.

De Vries had been accompanied by one of the men from the Watch. It was the same night that he had been grabbed while questioning the captain. De Vries and his companion brought candle lanterns, which cast shadows on their faces so that they looked like skulls.

De Vries sat down on a stool and said: 'So, Mr Bow Street Runner, you turn out to be a thief and a murderer.'

Blackstone said: 'Where's Hays?'

'That's none of your business.'

'I demand to see Hays, not one of his lackeys.'

'This', de Vries said softly, 'has nothing to do with Hays.'

'You mean you're acting in a ... private capacity.'

'Exactly.'

'You employed Laxton?'

The Dutchman's voice was flat, unemotional. 'There seems to be a mistake, Blackstone. We aren't here to answer your questions.'

Blackstone tested the ropes at his wrists. As tight as darbies. 'I'll only answer to Hays,' he said.

'He's not here and you'll answer to me. First of all, why did you break into Astor's house?' A note of reverence in his voice: his God wasn't at the altar, it was at the seat of money.

'That's a leading question, de Vries.'

'Answer it. Otherwise I shall have to resort to other methods. Methods which are distasteful to me.'

'I can't answer the question because I didn't break into Astor's home.'

'You lie,' said de Vries and Blackstone thought he sounded like a fanatical priest, a throwback from the Spanish Inquisition. 'I have proof.'

'Then you should take me to court.'

'I'm not interested in courts. Not in this case.'

'You're a bit of a villain, aren't you, de Vries. The worst sort – a hypocritical villain. Been to church today?'

'Hold your tongue.' De Vries turned to his companion, who was lounging against the wall. 'Show him we mean business, Young.'

Young hit Blackstone hard across the face twice, then kicked him in the ribs. Blackstone grunted and spat.

De Vries said: 'Why did you break into Astor's house?'

'What is it to you?'

'Why did you break in?'

'I don't admit breaking into anywhere and when I get out of here Hays will have your tripes for garters.'

'On the contrary, Hays is searching the city for *you*.'

'Then I hope to God he finds me.'

'Little chance of that, I'm afraid.' De Vries leaned forward, hands clasped in front of him as though praying. 'Why, Blackstone, why?'

Blackstone told de Vries to jump into the Hudson and cried out involuntarily as Young's fist banged his head against the wall. He slumped forward, momentarily stunned.

De Vries rocked back on the stool. 'All this is very distasteful to me. You might as well answer my questions – if, that is, you want to get out of here alive.'

'A pox on you,' Blackstone said as his head cleared.

De Vries held up his hand as Young went to hit Blackstone again. 'You're making it very hard for yourself. And it's all so unnecessary. Just tell me what I want to know and you can leave here.'

'Into the bay,' Blackstone said, 'tied to the barrel of a cannon.'

De Vries shrugged. 'Very well, I'll make it easier.' He hesitated. 'Supposing I told you I *knew* why you wanted to break into Astor's home?'

Blackstone said: 'Then I would wonder why the hell you've been asking me.'

A new quality entered de Vries's voice, thick and phlegmy. 'Supposing I told you I knew that you were after treasure.' He swallowed. 'Captain Kidd's treasure ... '

That was how the first interrogation had ended. Young gave him a couple more kicks and they both left, taking the stool with them.

Dawn entered the cell through the barred window, throwing a pattern on the flagstones. The air in the cell was foul and Blackstone could feel the heat gathering.

He slept a little, jerking awake every few minutes with the pain. He managed to stand up and jump around, but the rope burned his ankles. He looked for something to start fraying the ropes at his wrists, but there was nothing; and, in any case, he had always been sceptical about those tales in which the prisoner happens to find a sliver of broken glass or a jagged piece of metal with which to free himself. He sat down again and tried to untie the ropes round his ankles, but his wrists had been expertly bound and thin cord was knotted around his fingers and thumbs so that he couldn't move them.

He leaned against the wall, waited for the next move and analysed the events that had led up to his capture.

So de Vries knew about the treasure, presumably had always known about it. Was it he who had hired Laxton? The trouble is, Blackstone thought, that I've made so many enemies it's difficult to separate one plot from another.

He was sure that it was the captain of the frigate who had set the footpads on him. The captain had as good as admitted it. Then why had de Vries rescued him? Easy, Blackstone thought. He wanted me alive to answer his questions.

So it would seem that de Vries has always known what I was really after in New York...

A seagull perched on the ledge outside the barred window and peered in.

And then it came to him.

De Vries has always known what I was after – *even before I left London*. Because de Vries arranged it – de Vries suggested to Hays that I should come to New York in an advisory capacity.

Excitement stirred inside Blackstone. Excitement and chagrin, because he knew now that he had been manipulated ever since Fogarty had shown him the ruby.

De Vries had investigated the rumours about the foundation of Astor's wealth and decided they were true. He must have come across a ruby or some other gem that he had identified as being part of Kidd's loot.

But how to get his hands on the rest of the treasure without arousing suspicion in what was still a relatively small city? The obvious answer was to employ a villain.

Me!

Because it must have seemed a heaven-sent opportunity to de Vries when he heard that the Common Council had agreed with Hays's suggestion that they should invite a Bow Street Runner to New York.

De Vries must have heard about my reputation – God save me! At the very least it had been worth a try. The bait – one large, blood-red ruby shown to me by Fogarty, who must have been in the conspiracy. And why not? If de Vries got his hands on the treasure, then what better outlet in the future than Fogarty?

And they had played it cleverly. Both the ship's captain in London and the hotel thief being elusive ... me thinking I was outsmarting them ... Blackstone groaned aloud and the seagull flew away.

And the first person to feed me with the rumour about Astor's millions when I got to New York was ... of course ... de Vries.

But, as in most infallible plans, the unexpected occurred – I apparently failed to get further into Astor's home than the door at the end of the passage. De Vries must have reasoned that I couldn't have found any treasure or any clues to its whereabouts.

So why is he now trying to beat information out of me? Because he knows I returned to Astor's place in an official capacity. Because I'm a fugitive, because I might board a ship and get away for ever, because if Hays catches me he'll either have me locked up, where de Vries will be powerless to break my bones, or deport me – and then he'll never know if I discovered anything.

Then who hired Laxton?

There was only one answer, a process of elimination. From the moment he arrived, Blackstone had underestimated the opposition. I treated them like underprivileged colonials, he thought dismally. Telling Astor's financial adviser, Halleck, that I was a representative of *The Times*, presenting myself to Astor as a Bow Street Runner.

They must have thought I was a simpleton from the stews of London. Astor knew I was after his secrets, the duel was arranged...

God blind me!

Bolts rasped in the door and de Vries and Young returned for the second time.

'Hungry?' de Vries asked.

Blackstone shook his head, but his stomach whined in contradiction.

'I am.' Young, bow-legged and powerful, with a pockmarked face, handed de Vries a tray with soup, bread and cheese and a tankard of ale on it. De Vries began to eat.

'Thirsty?'

Blackstone shook his head, tongue dry in his mouth.

'Have you come to your senses?' de Vries asked, swigging from the tankard.

'Have you been to church yet?'

De Vries ignored him. 'You see we both know about Kidd's treasure. Now I'm prepared to do a deal with you.' De Vries stuffed some bread into his mouth. 'Tell me what you've found out and I'll split the swag with you.'

'I don't know what the hell you're talking about.'

De Vries drank some more ale. 'Oh yes you do, my friend. Fogarty told you, didn't he? And the good captain in London and – correct me if I'm mistaken – but I believe a certain hotel thief gave you some papers...'

Blackstone abandoned the pretence. 'He didn't *give* them to me.'

De Vries stopped chewing. 'He didn't?'

'I took them from his room.'

'Ah.'

'After he had been murdered.'

'You killed him?'

'A footpad killed him.'

'But you got the papers?'

'Yes,' Blackstone said, 'I got the papers.'

De Vries shook his head. 'Terrible, terrible, all this bloodshed and violence.' He paused to wipe his mouth with the back of his hand. 'Now tell me, what have you found out?'

'That you're a thief and a murderer.'

De Vries gestured to Young, who stepped forward and drove his fist into Blackstone's face. Blood poured from his nose and his head cracked against the wall.

'Thirsty work,' said de Vries, gulping down the last of the ale. 'Now, are you going to be sensible?'

Blackstone thrust himself forward and kicked up with his legs, knocked the tray out of de Vries's hands and fell on his back, lying there while Young kicked him four times in the belly.

De Vries held up his hand. 'That will be enough. We'll be back.'

And back they came, several times. Each time the same procedure, until the pain no longer mattered, only the thirst, as the day passed and the following night passed and the heat returned and they gave him enough water to keep him alive.

Blackstone estimated that it was about midday when they returned with a large roll of carpet. Blackstone stared at them, tongue swollen, eyes encrusted.

'Perhaps this will jog your memory,' de Vries said, unrolling the carpet and stepping primly aside as the body of Jacques Cartier was revealed.

De Vries said: 'We'll leave you two together for a little while – then perhaps you'll tell me about the map.'

Blackstone and Cartier stayed together for about an hour. Blackstone estimated that Cartier had been dead for about two days; he had been badly beaten; he stank and his sightless eyes stared directly at Blackstone.

De Vries, Blackstone thought, had at least learnt a method of interrogation from Hays.

Flies settled on Cartier's bloodied face.

If he had possessed the brains, he could have lived his days like a millionaire. Instead he had lived by the bottle and died at the hands of thugs.

The stench of the dead man grew stronger. Blackstone retched and choked; his tongue was a gag stuck in his mouth. He shut his eyes. The map, the bloody map. That was why they were still interrogating him. What could he tell them about it? It was printed on his memory, but where the hell was it? South America, Australia, Africa... He lost consciousness.

He was in the arms of Fanny Campbell... he was striding down Bow Street on his first day as a Runner, cocksure and with a spring in his step... he was on the gallows, the noose round his neck – the gallows, always the gallows...

The door opened ... the noose clutched his neck and he opened his eyes to find de Vries's hand round his throat, shaking him.

De Vries said: 'Well?'

Blackstone, jerked back from the bottomless well of death, croaked.

'Give him some water,' de Vries said.

Young thrust a beaker of water to Blackstone's lips. Blackstone drank greedily.

'Enough.' De Vries pushed Young's hand away and said to Blackstone again: 'Well?' Again Blackstone croaked, aware that he had found a way of getting more water.

The beaker was back at his lips. He drank and then croaked again, but this time de Vries said: 'Enough – he's play-acting.' He pointed at Cartier's body: 'Do you want to end up like that?'

Blackstone shook his head. An academic question – no one wanted to end up like that.

'Then tell me about the map. Tell me what you found out about Astor, but first of all tell me about the map.'

'What map?'

This time de Vries hit him, with the back of his hand across the cheek, jerking Blackstone's head sideways. 'You know what map. Cartier told us he'd given you one ... '

'Then why didn't you ask *him* about it?'

'Because he died before we had time to. This' – gesturing contemptuously at Young – 'dolt hit him too hard.'

Young hung his head.

'I don't know anything about a map.'

De Vries's voice rose to a shriek. Saliva dribbled down his chin. 'The map, I want the map.'

There was no point in pretending any longer. But at least there ought to be a grain of pleasure left in this life, so

Blackstone said: 'I destroyed it.' He enjoyed the expression on de Vries's face.

'You did what?'

'I destroyed it.' Blackstone savoured the last enjoyment he would experience.

'You stupid bastard.'

'Watch that language,' Blackstone said.

'Can you remember what the map looked like?'

Blackstone said: 'I might if I had some more water.'

'Give him more water.'

Again the beaker of life at his lips. Blackstone sucked the water down.

'Well?'

'I've forgotten.'

De Vries drew a pistol from his belt. 'Remember, my friend. If you value your life, remember.'

'Even if I did, I don't know where the island is.'

'I might.' De Vries cocked the pistol. 'So remember!'

'Now let's see,' Blackstone said, acknowledging the unplumbed depths of his fear and wondering at the calm voice that he could hear issuing from his lips.

De Vries prodded him between the eyes with the pistol. 'Remember!'

But Blackstone was saved the effort. Because at that moment the bars of the window disappeared. And so did half the wall.

Three masked men leapt into the gaping hole.

De Vries turned and fired but, as his finger squeezed the trigger of his flintlock, the first man through the hole struck his hand down. The ball tore a hole in the chest of long-dead Cartier.

The butt of another pistol descended on the back of de Vries's neck. He fell to his knees, then slumped forward on his face.

Young fought briefly, then joined de Vries on the floor.

The man who had hit de Vries took off his mask. 'Good afternoon,' said Billy the Boston cracksman.

Blackstone smiled. And fainted.

Billy threw the contents of the beaker in his face. 'Hey, come on, we've got to get you out of here.'

Blackstone regained consciousness. He was icy cold despite the heat. He felt sick. He said: 'How...?'

They cut his bonds with knives and Billy said: 'Simple, I have friends on the Watch. They told me what happened the other night. And it wasn't too difficult to find out where you had been staying.' The burglar stuck his hand in his pocket. 'We searched your room and found this.' He handed Blackstone a ruby. 'This must be the first time I've ever returned stolen property.'

Blackstone stared at the ruby he had found in Astor's jewel case. 'I don't know what—'

'Then don't,' Billy interrupted. 'And get moving, we haven't much time...'

Blackstone stood up, and fell down again.

The cracksman kneeled down and massaged Blackstone's wrists and ankles; diamonds sparkled on his cuffs and fingers. 'A neat job, eh?' He nodded his head towards the hole. 'Just the way we did it in Boston. Four good strong horses, never known to fail. I never did trust that bastard de Vries – too holy to be true. I guessed he had brought you here.'

'Here?'

The cracksman grinned. 'Yes, here – you're under a church, my friend. The last place on God's earth anyone would think of looking for you. Except Billy boy,' he added. 'We kept watch on de Vries's house and followed him here.'

Blackstone felt stronger. 'But why did you do this?'

The cracksman shrugged. 'Because a lady asked me, and I never could resist a lady. God knows why, though. If you had snuffed it, then I might have stood a chance ... '

'How can I repay you?'

'The ruby?'

Blackstone handed it to him, but Billy thrust it into Blackstone's pocket. 'You're going to need some money, my friend. Perhaps one day I'll come to London – then you can repay me. Perhaps a map of the vaults of the Bank of England?' He chuckled. 'Now we'd best get you to a ship before Hays and his men get wind of this. You know, a hole torn in the side of a church can attract attention.'

Blackstone stood up and walked a few steps, picking his way between the bodies lying on the floor.

The cracksman said: 'There's a horse waiting for you outside. Make for Whitehall Slip. There's a rowboat there. Make for a sloop called the *Daphne*, anchored right in front of you. You can't miss her.'

Blackstone stuck out his hand. 'Thanks.'

'Don't thank me, thank Fanny Campbell.'

'Aye,' Blackstone said, 'she's saved my life twice.'

He emerged into the street just as Hays and three members of the Watch rounded a corner, three hundred yards away.

Blackstone hurled himself on to the waiting horse. No sense in heading for Whitehall Slip: they'd catch him as he boarded the rowboat, and even if they didn't, they'd shoot him down as he made for the sloop.

Blackstone touched the horse with his heels and prayed that he was made of the same stuff as his own horse, Poacher.

Through a maze of streets, on to Greenwich Street. Afternoon strollers leaping out of his way. A pistol shot, the slurring sound of a ball passing over his head.

The horse moved as if it were bred for racing. Blackstone gripped as hard as he could with his thighs, but that wasn't very hard, not in his condition. He felt dizzy and he had to blink away the crusts from his eyes. Houses... cottages... hedgerows...

Another shot.

Then he saw the balloon, and the crowd gathered around it. In the basket stood Fanny, an imperious figure in yellow dress and bonnet. There had been four ropes holding the balloon: three had been cut, and the great dimpled bulk was tugging strongly at the last one.

'Hey there!' Blackstone shouted, as the horse galloped into the field. The crowd scattered, another ball passed over his head, just missing the balloon. 'Hey there!' Blackstone shouted to Fanny.

He rode straight up to the basket, leapt off the horse while it was still at the gallop, fell, picked himself up and vaulted into the basket. 'Good afternoon,' he said. 'Let's get this thing off the ground.'

Behind them Hays and his men entered the field, pistols in their hands.

Fanny shouted to a man standing beside a tree to which the fourth length of rope was tied. 'Let it go.' He stared back at her dazedly. 'Let it go, damn you.'

Hays was almost on the basket. The rope parted from the tree and the basket began to rise. But slowly. So slowly. Hays clawed at the basket and Blackstone grabbed a sandbag and clubbed his hands with it. Hays fell to the ground. Fanny was busy throwing sandbags overboard.

Hays grabbed the pistol he had dropped when Blackstone hit his hands and shouted: 'I'll shoot it down. One shot and down you come.'

Blackstone peered over the basket. 'And murder the girl?'

Suddenly the balloon took off, accelerating upwards at great speed. Above tree level, up, up... Blackstone heard a shot; he didn't know whether Hays was aiming at the balloon or not; but the ball missed.

And then they were drifting out towards the Hudson and the people with the upturned faces beneath them were pygmies and they were together in the blue vault of the skies.

He must have fainted again. Because the next thing he knew was that his head was cradled in her lap and she was bending down and kissing him.

He tried to smile. 'So you saved me again?'

'We've each done it twice,' she said. 'That's the way it should be. Equality, you see.' She kissed him again.

'Here,' he said, 'I've got a present for you,' handing her the ruby. 'Worth a fortune I shouldn't wonder.' And then: 'Where are we going by the way?'

She stood up and gazed over the side of the basket. Beneath was the broad passage of the Hudson, molten in the sunlight. 'We seem', she told him, 'to be heading towards Canada.'

Then it arrived – the breeze for which swooning New York had been waiting for so long. It was a young and frisky breeze, coming down from the North. But it grew precociously – strapping youngster... strong adult...

It gathered the balloon in its grasp and sent it back in the direction it had come. Out towards the Atlantic.

'So what do we do?' Blackstone asked.

'We can't let the gas out now,' she said. 'It would be too dangerous.'

'I agree,' Blackstone said. 'It might drop me into Hays's outstretched arms.'

'Then all we can do is pray.'

Blackstone nodded and put his arm round her. As they passed over Manhattan Toe, Blackstone glanced down to his right. There was Liberty Island. 'Good God!' Blackstone exclaimed.

'What is it?'

Blackstone pointed down. 'That's the island.'

'What island? What are you talking about?'

Blackstone told her about the map. 'And that's it all right. That's where the bulk of Captain Kidd's treasure is buried. Perhaps one day I'll come back for it,' he said, thoughtfully. 'If, that is, we ever come down again.'

'Funny people, the Americans,' Fanny said 'Who knows, they might build on top of the treasure. A church, a monument, even a statue...'

At dawn next morning the skipper of the packet bound for Liverpool pointed at a balloon descending towards the ship. 'Looks like we've got more passengers,' he said to no one in particular.

Printed in Poland
by Amazon Fulfillment
Poland Sp. z o.o., Wrocław